THE
BEAUTIFUL
SOMETHING
ELSE

Also by

ASH VAN OTTERLOO

Cattywampus

A Touch of Ruckus

THE BEAUTIFUL SOMETHING ELSE

ASH VAN OTTERLOO

Scholastic Press * New York

Library of Congress Cataloging-in-Publication Data
Names: Van Otterloo, Ash, author.
Title: The beautiful something else / by Ash Van Otterloo.
Description: New York : Scholastic Press, 2023. | Audience: Ages 8–12. | Audience: Grades 4–6. | Summary: When Sparrow's mother is sent to rehab for opioid addiction, Sparrow is sent to live in a commune with her estranged aunt where Sparrow begins to embrace their true gender identity.
Identifiers: LCCN 2022028663 | ISBN 9781338843224 (hardcover) | ISBN 9781338843248 (ebook)
Subjects: LCSH: Gender identity—Juvenile fiction. | Gender nonconformity—Juvenile fiction. | Mothers and daughters—Juvenile fiction. | Children of drug abusers—Juvenile fiction. | Aunts—Juvenile fiction. | Communal living—Juvenile fiction. | CYAC: Gender identity—Fiction. | Gender nonconformity—Fiction. | Mothers and daughters—Fiction. | Drug abuse—Fiction. | Aunts—Fiction. | Communal living—Fiction. | LCGFT: Novels.
Classification: LCC PZ7.1.V38 Sp 2023 | DDC 813.6 [Fic]—dc23/eng/20220718
LC record available at https://lccn.loc.gov/2022028663

10 9 8 7 6 5 4 3 2 1   23 24 25 26 27

Printed in Italy   183
First edition, May 2023

Book design by Cassy Price

To my younger self and the clever breadcrumb
trail you left all the way back to your soul.
You did good, kiddo.

A Note from the Author

I believe the world needs all kind of stories—happy, sad, funny, realistic, and ones that show us what the world might look like if we all loved and valued one another a little bit more. This story is (hopefully!) a combination of all of these.

While many LGBTQIA+ kids grow up supported, many live in situations where people don't accept them as they are (or simply don't know how to). While writing *The Beautiful Something Else*, I wanted to explore a gradual, realistic identity discovery similar to that of many nonbinary and trans people. This includes some difficult moments, like when Sparrow's mom has a hard time recognizing and respecting these changes, mostly by using Sparrow's deadname (a name that isn't their chosen name) and not honoring Sparrow's gender expression. This can be upsetting for some people to read, so I wanted to provide a heads-up and remind you to always be kind to yourself.

Other possibly sensitive content for *The Beautiful Something Else* includes substance addiction in an adult, mention of off-page abuse and neglect, misgendering, and implied homophobia.

If a story ever starts feeling a little too heavy as you read,

I want to remind you it's okay to put it down for a while. (Or forever, even!) You might also find it helpful to process your thoughts with a trusted adult who supports you.

I've done my best to pack this book with hope, too: LGBTQIA+ joy, humor, shared community, found family, resilience, a fierce love of nature and natural science, and, most of all, deep acceptance. I hope it brings you as a reader as much pride and healing as I felt while writing it. Keep shining, and always remember that everything about you is worthy of celebration and respect.

All my love,
Ash Van Otterloo

Chapter One
Sparrow, Disrupted

Sparrow Malone

Mrs. Garcia

English Language Arts Homework, Purple

Mimicry in Nature

Animals don't mean to lie about who they are. It's how they're wired. The anglerfish didn't wake up one day in the deep sea and think to herself, "You know what? Today, I'll hang a lantern on my head and lure my neighbors to their death." Millions of years ago, the first anglerfish accidentally caught a bacteria that caused her dorsal fins to bioluminesce.

1

Then evolution did its thing over many generations, and the fish became mimics, luring their prey with glowing bait-like appendages. The anglerfish doesn't even know she's a trickster—she just knows that she needs to survive . . .

Mom is in rare form this morning, and I don't need to go downstairs to know it.

From my room, I can hear the metallic *shhhhlink* of our little apartment's old, dusty blinds opening and closing, over and over. Every time a siren wails or muffled voices travel down our complex's rain-slick sidewalk, my mother peeps through the window to see what's happening. I try to shut out the noise as I scribble the last bit of my English homework and scan it for errors.

Shhhhhlink!! My face scrunches in exasperation. *Who does she expect to see out there anyway?* I give up and slide my homework into my backpack. I can finish the proofread at school. The front door whines open and shut as Mom steps out onto the stoop. Seconds later, sweet-smelling vape smoke dances up from the scraggly boxwoods and past my open window like dragon breath. I roll my eyes. So much for her quitting.

Today's too important for me to get caught in one of Mom's whirlpool moods. I need my game face on for my first language arts presentation at Candy Creek Middle School. Turning her angst into a silly game usually helps. I relax my neck and let my voice slide to the deepest end of its register, imitating the famous nature documentarian David Attenborough.

"Like a groundhog on the first day of spring, the wild Nervous Mom peeps out of its habitation, checking for predators," I narrate as I paw through the mound of laundry at the foot of my bed. "Meanwhile, inside their cramped domain, her offspring busies itself with its never-ending search for suitable clothing," I continue, switching up my accent to sound more like Ze Frank, my favorite silly nature YouTuber. *"And that's how the Malone family do."*

Other ways of the Malone family include Mom working irregular shifts, this month as a companion for elderly folks. She changes jobs a lot. I've only been at Candy Creek for three weeks, since she left her last one because a coworker saw her crying in the grocery store after she'd had too much to drink.

Don't get me wrong, Mom's a hard worker—we both are. It's just that her anxious perfectionism and her messy personal life go together like Cheetos and milk. Eventually, she melts down in public or makes a huge mistake, and she quits because she's too mortified to ever go back.

So today, I, Sparrow, need to make an excellent impression on new teachers so Mom looks good, and folks won't get nosy about her twelve-year-old being home alone at night while she works.

I cast a longing look at my ratty, oversized gray Wolverine sweatshirt in the corner, wishing it were chilly enough outside to disappear inside it. Paired with flip-flops and shorts, it's my favorite outfit. It's comfortable like a blanket, and the furthest Mom lets me stray from girly clothes without flipping her lid, if she's in a good mood. Today she clearly isn't, though, so I'm tempting fate here.

Plus, even if it weren't a million sticky Southern degrees outside already, *despite* the rain, I might not get away with wearing it to this school. Candy Creek Middle has a loose-but-official dress code of khaki pants and polos. And this year, since I now wear the same size clothes as my tiny mom, I've been rotating through her hand-me-downs from her last job at the Dollar Saver, to cut corners. But today, if I have to wear them one more time, I feel like I might scream.

My sweatshirt is halfway over my head when Mom tops the stairs and passes my bedroom. "Oh, honey, you are *not* wearing that raggedy mess."

"Plenty of people break dress code," I complain, my voice smothered under a layer of cotton. "Two girls in my class wore dresses and sandals yesterday!"

"Well, I imagine they looked *nice*, not like a sack of potatoes," Mom scoffs before shuffling away again, her voice trailing off. "Wouldn't kill you to try a dress sometime."

"Not likely," I mutter, but Mom's already gone.

The room whirls a little as I obediently discard my sweatshirt. My pulse skitters, and my guts feel like I'm on a fast elevator. I hate changing clothes—maybe because it means I'm officially headed to school and I'm nervous?—so I rush through it as quickly as possible. Wrinkling my nose at the way the stretchy lilac fabric hugs my body, I paw my long red hair forward like a safety blanket. I wish I had time to flip it all over my face, too, and pretend to be Samara from *The Ring*, a terrifying movie I regret watching while Mom was at work, but my alarm clock already reads seven thirty. The door creaks open and shut downstairs. Better hurry.

I twist my hair into wholesome braids that say, "I make good grades, eat organic beans, and I'll never smoke, chew, or kiss boys who do!" As my fingers work, I picture someone cutting the hair off at my shoulder, my chin, and all the way up to my ears. *Snip, snip, SNIP.* A shiver sneaks down my back. I glance over my shoulder, neck burning with irrational embarrassment like I've been caught picking my nose.

Mom's back in the doorway, watching me with that fragile, too-bright smile on her face. Her sleek ponytail is impeccable as always, with only the barest hint of her graying roots showing beneath her chocolate-brown drugstore dye job. She's dressed for work, perfectly pressed and neat as a pin, her hands gripping her scuffed pocketbook hard. But I detect the telltale tremble in her fingers anyway, and her lip is bleeding from chewing it too much. She's still wound up. "I wish you wouldn't slouch that way—it makes you look like an old man. D'you have all your homework done, Maggie Grace?"

"I don't know about Maggie Grace, but *Sparrow* does," I sing, ignoring her dig and slipping into my shoes to putter over and kiss her cheek.

Mom sighs through her nose. "I named you Magnolia Grace after the tree I loved as a girl—" she starts in. The pinprick irises of her green eyes scrutinize my hair, her thin-plucked brows fretting.

"Where you climbed up to escape your horrible, smelly brother and that lonely house where you were raised up," I finish for her, forcing a laugh. Because we've repeated this talk googolplex times—a number so big, you could never write it out in a life span. I roll my eyes, herding us out of my room with my fraying bookbag. "Sparrow's easier for new folks to remember." *And it's the one thing that's really mine*, I think. I love the feel of *Sparrow* in my mouth, wild and strong.

"It's just so weird, Maggie. I worry folks will get the wrong idea about us. They might think you're . . . well, it just sounds a little *funny*." Her gaze is a cloud of worry, worry, worry, roaming over my body and searching for something to rain on. "Why do you keep wearing that old tight sports bra? You know it makes you look flat as a flitter—" My jaw clenches, but Mom doesn't notice, just keeps going. "Didn't we buy you that nice one with the cups in it? And, your eyebrows are looking a little wild . . . let me grab my tweezers, quick—"

I take a step back, fighting the urge to snarl. Sometimes, my mom's worse than the unsettling feeling I get from the mirror. "Mom, *stop*. It's fine! We don't want to be late, right?"

"Oh, shoot, I guess you're right—it's 7:32 . . ."

Mom teeters on her feet in a way I don't like. She's taken something, I can tell—a sleeping pill, maybe? I pretend not to see, but when her back turns and I follow her down the stairwell and out to the car, I bite my lip. *I'm about to get on the road with this woman.* Bless her, but Mom doesn't need to be behind a wheel sometimes. Only four more years before I can drive us on days like this.

"How do you feel about that English class thingy your teacher emailed about?" Mom asks as our respective car doors clunk shut. "You stuck to writing about . . . nice things, didn't you?"

She's trying to sound casual, but instead her tone is like brittle candy, ready to shatter. I know what her question really means. She's not wondering if I feel confident. She's asking: *Will your teacher like it? Will she be impressed by how mature you are? Will they think I'm a good mom? That we're good folks?*

I nod, smiling. "I feel great about it. One of my best yet."

My mom's face brightens the tiniest bit as she cranks the

car and pulls out of the driveway. I wish I could reach over to smooth my thumbs over her beautiful forehead and erase all the worry lines that congregate there. But that would smear her carefully applied makeup and reveal the smattering of freckles underneath, causing her to spontaneously combust.

"And are you going out for any solos this year? Or musicals?" Mom's Tennessee accent is rolling in thicker, and her words are slurring a little. "I don't want you . . . chickening out this time. Not when I know you're sittin' on all that natural talent. You'll try harder for your mama, won't you?"

I swallow hard and hesitate. I don't say that the stage makes me nervous, or that all this adjusting is tougher than it looks. Because I *need* Mom to be okay right now. She's already starting to get cagey, and we've only been in Candy Creek a few weeks. In the corner of my eye, I see her pocket-book unzipped on the floorboard, and my gaze is pulled as if by gravity. And, sure enough, my heart skips at the sliver of a plastic zip baggie inside.

Mom approaches a red light a little too fast, slamming the brakes down hard at the last minute. I snap my eyes back upward. We both lurch forward and are caught by our seat belts. Mom gasps down air in surprise, her bony chest heaving and threader earrings still swinging. "Well, *that'll* wake us up!" She chuckles nervously, then looks around the intersection to see if anyone saw us skid a little past the crosswalk line.

But me? I'm staring at the plastic baggie that has fallen all the way out of Mom's purse onto the carpeted floorboard. It's full of familiar little white circles with lines on them, like flathead screw tops made of chalk. The medicine Mom took a couple years back, after her thumb was crushed on a car assembly line in South Carolina. The ones she's not supposed to take anymore, because her thumb hasn't hurt her for ages. *How'd she get ahold of them again?* Mom finally checks to see if I'm okay and notices me staring at her bag. I jerk my attention politely to the window, heart racing.

"Sweet old Mr. Hemphill left his heart pills in my car after I drove him to his checkup," Mom chirps. Her smile's too big, like she can't remember how many teeth a person shows when they're honestly happy. Fifteen? Twenty? *All of them?* "I need to remember to put them back in his cabinet."

"Better write it down, so you don't forget!" I wag my finger in mock sternness. Inside, I want to pummel the dashboard with the heels of my shoes, over and over. *Heart pills, my butt.* Instead, I twist the radio knob and groove to the beat, waggling my brows at Mom until she gives in and laughs. She's lying about the medicine, and we both know it.

I shouldn't be hurt—I already suspected. She loves the stuffing out of me, and we're as close as Bonnie and Clyde. We're all each other has. But there's stuff we just don't talk about.

It's better that way. Back when she used to drink every night, tearful, broken-edged words poured from her like water. I didn't know how to handle them, because we didn't have rules for Mama being honest.

"My shadow's chasing me again, Maggie Grace," she'd sob, curled into a tiny ball on the sofa. "We can't stop movin', baby girl." And Mom never meant "We can't stop moving" in the fun "can't stop, won't stop groovin'" T-Swift sort of way. She meant find a new town, burn old bridges, make another start.

First time Mom said it, I'd just read about a creature called the Hidebehind in a school library book. The folklore, it said, originated in North America. Legend went, the evil Hidebehind stalked lumberjacks through forests thick and dark, matching their every step. But when they turned around, the Hidebehind disappeared behind the nearest tree. Some folks believed keeping a little flask of moonshine with you kept the Hidebehind at bay.

In my eight-year-old noggin, Mom's shadow and the Hidebehind got mixed up, and I thought the Hidebehind was why Mom took so many drinks and medicine she didn't need. Mom's shadow was real enough to me then, and still is now—a sticky, sad secret she can't ever shake off, following us everywhere.

Mom's quiet the rest of the way to school. As we pull up to the drop-off line, my toes curl up hard inside my shoes, tiny hidden turtles of anxiety. But my posture straightens, and I force a relaxed, sweet expression onto my face.

"I'm thinking of tryin' out for choir. Miss H heard me singing in the hall, and said she has a spot for a voice good as mine, if I want it." This is Sparrow-and-Mom code for: *Please don't fall apart, Mom. I know it's hard. If you hang in there, I'll give you something to brag about to your new coworkers and church choir members, so they know you're a perfectly normal, highly successful mom.*

Mom smiles a little. It's small this time but real. "We'll have to fix you up a dress for concerts, Maggie Grace. And you'll have to actually *wear* it."

I cringe inside at the dreaded name and think *Sparrow!!* But I grin, too. I can already see the wheels whirring in Mom's head about the cheapest place to buy clothes, and how she can make them glitzier. My toes uncurl a little.

Busy is good. Her green eyes are sparking with Mom-fire, and she looks almost alert.

If I can distract her with concerts and grades, maybe her itchy feet will settle in. She'll see that folks really do like us. We can conjure a sunshine life so bright, Mom's Hidebehind shadow might disappear for good. I'll go through her purse and hurl every last baggie into the dumpster, if I have to.

"Love you! Do good!"

"I love you, too, Mom. Pick me up at four!"

As she drives away, I whisper, "C'mon, sunshine."

Chapter Two

Sparrow Blending In

Sparrow Malone

Mrs. Garcia

ELA Homework, Purple

Mimicry in Nature

Some scientists have concluded Indonesian mimic octopuses are intelligent disguise artists. Mimic octopuses observe their surroundings and react creatively to fool prey and predators alike. Folding its legs back, the mimic octopus can impersonate a flounder, gliding across the naked ocean floor. It's a contortion artist who can configure itself into the shape of a venomous lionfish claiming its freedom in open water. When bullied by aggressive fish, it shifts to imitate a deadly sea snake, Jedi-mind-trick-style. "I am not the octopus you're looking for." It transforms into whatever the situation calls for, which makes it a master of survival.

It's a creative problem solver, but it's hard to say whether it has a conscience like people do . . .

As I walk down the sheltered sidewalk from the drop-off line to the school's entrance, the bottom falls out of the sky and rain lashes the parking lot in blurry sheets. Outside on the ground, the wet, hot pavement swirls with oily rainbows. I wait for a moment, breathing in deep. I adore rain.

I resist the urge to peel off my clothes and dance in the downpour until I'm clammy and shriveled, the way I did when I was small. Instead, I gingerly stick my hand out from beneath the awning's protection right into the deluge and start walking. Electric joy sparks through me as cold drops pelt and sting the skin on my hand and wrist, and I stifle a whoop.

Twenty seconds. That's how long I have to myself

between being supportive Mom-Sparrow and shape-shifting school-Sparrow. I'm usually last in the car line, so I get this stretch of gum-stained cement to myself. It's my rule: no worrying about Mom, no worrying about school on the sidewalk. Clearing my head is my good-luck charm.

My walk slows to a saunter, and I like the strange, almost cocky rhythm of it. It's almost a swagger. Who *is* this twenty-second Sparrow? The question puts a weird, squirming sensation in my belly, and I let the roar of water battering metal drown out my thoughts. Steam rises from the slick blacktop, kissing my chin. *Ten, nine, eight, seven, six, five, four, three* . . .

Annnnd showtime.

School-Sparrow takes over as my dripping hand pushes open the door to Candy Creek Middle. The smell of wet dirt and steaming pavement gives way to a whirlwind of twelve different Bath and Body Works sprays, plus the tang of disinfectant cleaner and burnt pizza.

Eyes sharp, my swagger disappears. Shifting my backpack, I hurry down the main hallway and narrowly miss colliding with two boys trying and failing to run up the cinderblock walls, parkour-style. I scowl, heart pounding, as a bearded teacher hollers for them to knock it off. The boys hang their heads, snickering sheepishly before rounding the corner and starting up again. Part of me wants to stick a leg out and trip them, because—*hello*—inconsiderate and boneheaded menaces to society. But, with burning cheeks, I realize another part of me wants to show them how it's done. I want to whoop so loud folks hear me coming and scurry to the side to watch. My competitive streak fantasizes about seeing their eyes go wide with admiration. *Whoa, sick! Do that again!!* Which is ridiculous, because I would never risk a teacher yelling at me. Also, these old shoes don't have nearly enough tread on them to create that kind of friction.

"Are you okay, sweetheart?" Bearded Teacher asks. Eighth-grade science, I think?

I tent my eyebrows in an expression of shared exasperation. I nod with a nice, strong chin. I'm a sensible-yet-startled student grateful for the concern. He chuckles and rolls his eyes knowingly. "They'll have more sense when they're older, don't worry."

Not knowing what to say, I fake a laugh and keep moving.

I jog up the stairs and wind through corridors until I

reach Mrs. Garcia's language arts classroom, just in time to hear her calling attendance. I pause at the door to catch my breath, but Mrs. Garcia spots me and waves me inside with a patient, no-nonsense smile. She's only on Emma Barney's name, so I'm not that late. *Good.*

Scuttling to my seat, I pull out my fat report folder and assume a "blend in" posture. Not secretly playing skateboard games on my phone under the table, like my restless desk mate, Drew, but also not paying such rapt attention that I'll get teased. That's happened before. *I just need to wait my turn and nail my essay presentation,* I think, running my fingers across my overstuffed writing binder for luck. Inside it is every A-plus essay I've ever written. Not just in this class or for this grade year, either. Like, *all* of them. *Is it weird that I keep all my old papers together?* I wonder. No one else does. But I like the way they wind like one long thread through all the places me and Mom have ever lived, connecting them. They remind me that no matter where I go, I can count on my brain to do its thing.

When Mrs. Garcia calls the first student of the day to come present, my focus zooms in. A tall girl in a red sweater—Prisha, I think—has written a poem about butterfly migration for her free write. Her verses are so elegant

I want to soak them in. But instead, I home in on Mrs. Garcia's face and study her reactions. My teacher seems especially impressed by Prisha's confident, strong voice. Every time Prisha emphasizes a word with passion, Mrs. Garcia's eyes sparkle behind her glasses. Good to know.

Sliding my folder aside, I plant my elbows on the table. Two more presentations clue me in that Mrs. Garcia appreciates humor and impeccable manners. I'm embarrassed for sucking up this hard, and usually, my work is so solid I don't need to. But I see that plastic bag tumble from Mom's purse again and again in my mind. If I'm going to turn things around for Mom and me, I need to start performing my heart out.

Drew snickers beside me, but I ignore him. He bumps my elbow, and I ignore him again. Finally, he whispers not-so-quietly, "Oh my god. 'How cauliflower farts can be used as alternative rocket fuel'? Is this your paper?"

I feel all the blood drain out of my face. *My folder is open on the table.* I look over and see Drew's dirty-fingernail hands clutching the oldest essay from my binder—a science hypothesis that's only embarrassing if you don't know I wrote it when I was eight. If Drew were observant at all, he'd have noticed the date. And the way he's sneering, his hot cheese breath four inches from my face, tells me everything. He thinks I'm a too-weird, too-gross girl—just the way my classmates saw me in third grade. This—plus the fact that Mom and I change towns often—is why I never bother with friends. Something inside me comes unraveled, and I can hear my angry heartbeat thrumming.

"Give it *back*." My voice is wobbling. I'm not used to being angry in front of people. I don't even know how to hold my angry body, and I'm embarrassed by the way my hands are shaking. So, I imagine I'm Gandalf fighting the Balrog—my eyebrows are diving ravens and I'm squaring up and leaning into Drew's space.

"But it's hilarious." He laughs, holding it up out of my reach and leaning back in his chair. "*You're* hilarious!"

My brain faintly registers Mrs. Garcia's voice calling our names, but some wild and raw feeling takes over me, and all rational thoughts evaporate. Muscles in my jaw clench and I growl. Then I plant the sole of my shoe right on the edge of Drew's chair and *kick*.

The minute he lands on the carpet, I snap out of it, mortified at what I've done. Drew doesn't seem hurt—in fact, he's shrieking with laughter. "You're crazy, girl!" Several kids cover their mouths, and Drew's buddies hoot and take pictures on their phones. I take in Mrs. Garcia's shocked face, and my skin swirls with hot and cold at once. I feel exposed. It feels a lot like falling.

Before Mrs. Garcia can say anything, though, the classroom telephone rings. She holds up a finger for me to stay put while she has a hushed conversation with whoever's on the other line. I wait. Everyone stares, and my body feels weird.

I mumble, "I'm so sorry. I think I'm gonna be sick," just before I run from the room, shoes squeaking.

In the bathroom, I cough and gag over the toilet. I didn't eat breakfast, so there's not much to it. My face burns. I wish I could cry, but my tear ducts are rusty plumbing. How did I get from my sidewalk to *here*? Mrs. Garcia will send me to the office, no doubt. *Please don't let them call Mom*, I pray to literally any deity who will listen. The office may think calling Mom will straighten me out, help me deal. But folks don't get that's not how Mom and I work—there's a certain balance to us, a fragile teeter-totter rhythm, and usually I'm the one keeping it.

I sit on the plastic commode seat and stay there until I'm sure class is over, naming off collective nouns in my head to drown out the worry. *An obstinacy of buffalo. An embarrassment of pandas. A smack of jellyfish. A flock of sparrows . . .*

Finally, the bathroom door squeaks open. "Sparrow? Are you in here?" Mrs. Garcia's voice doesn't seem harsh or angry, but I still want to flush myself to oblivion.

"Yeah."

"Mija, I need you to come down to the office with me."

Of course. Sheepish, I emerge from the stall. I try to keep my eyes glued on the ground, but I steal a glance at my teacher out of habit. *What must she think of me? Can I fix it?* Mrs. Garcia's normally sharp golden eyes are pools of gentle concern. That's like a hot knife, right to the soul, and my face crumples. "I'm so sorry for what I did, Mrs. Garcia. I'll never do it again. I know it was disrespectful and awful, and I—"

"I know, Sparrow, I know. But listen, I need you to come with me quickly." It's then I notice Mrs. Garcia's holding *all* my school things in her arms. She's even gathered my potted spider plant project from science class. Why does this look like it's my last day of school? Dread **gath**ers in my belly, cold and tight.

Am I being banished because I kicked Drew's chair? *Oh no. Oh please no.* That would destroy Mom. Mrs. Garcia's face pinches like some adults' do when they think something's a real shame. Like she's sorry for me. I brace myself for the terrible words that will absolutely ruin my life. But it does nothing to prepare me for what comes next.

"I'm so sorry, sweetheart. But we got a call. Something's happened with your mom."

Chapter Three
Sparrow All Alone

Sparrow's notebook

There is no technically correct collective noun for a group of octopuses, or if there ever was, it's gone dusty past recognition from lack of use. There's nothing like "murder" or "flock" or "murmuration" or "pride" or "swarm," like you use for birds, mammals, or insects. Those animals are communal, whereas the octopus is solitary. It faces the vast ocean alone. So it doesn't need a collective noun.

I'm in the front seat of an old Jetta with a snoring pug in my lap, next to a woman who looks a little like me—same red hair, same sunburned face, same grass-green eyes. But we're practically strangers. I guess technically, we're not even related. This is my Aunt Mags, Uncle Cameron's wife, who no one ever told me about. Married to the uncle Mom hates, who I've never met.

As wooded farms whiz by, the past few days blur in my mind except for painful flashes of memory:

Mrs. Garcia squeezing my hand while a social worker tells me Mom's had a car accident and is in the hospital. That while she's okay, Mom's taken too much medicine and needs lots of help recovering, for a couple days at the hospital and then for at least a month in rehabilitation.

An aunt I've never met arriving late at night with a giant chocolate cake and her dog, Bela Pugosi, who has an underbite. Me, latching on to Bela and not letting go while he licked the quiet tears off my face during my last nights at home.

Watching movies on the couch for three days, because my aunt promised we wouldn't have to leave Mom's and my apartment until I decided I was ready.

Aunt Mags packing a bag for me the morning I said it was okay, and another bag to send to Mom, who isn't coming to Mags's house with us. Me, fiddling with my shoelaces while Mags explained Mom has an illness called addiction, *which I already understood.*

Aunt Mags telling me I'm staying at Windy Hall while Mom is in rehabilitation at a care facility nearby, and that we can visit her when she's well enough for visitors.

I'm wrung out of tears, but my heart drops every time I picture Mom in a hospital bed alone. I cringe at how embarrassed and keyed up she must be. Everything's weird. And being in the car with Mags? It's nothing like riding with Mom.

The trouble with Aunt Mags is, she doesn't seem to *need* anything. Even though she's older than Mom by a lot, with poppy-colored hair shot through with silver ribbons, she seems decades younger. Mags's hair is wound up into two massive buns with butterflies pinned to the centers. Her tank top is tastefully low-cut, she wears several necklaces, and every last inch of her is dusted with fine lines and freck-les. But it's mostly her mannerisms that throw me off—so maddeningly calm, they're impossible to read. *How do I act around you, lady?*

"It's been a while since you ate. Anything sound good for dinner, kiddo?" Mags asks in her soft alto voice.

I bite my lip. *The displaced Malone offspring studies its*

caregiver tentatively, uncertain of how to proceed, I narrate in my head. *The adolescent must act wisely, adapting to its caregiver's sensibilities, in order to survive.* It's what I always do.

The thing is? The more I study Mags's expressions for hints, the more I have no clue how to act—which version of myself to be. She just hums away with the radio, off-key and serene, as farm grass undulates in the wind outside. Which should annoy me given the circumstances, but somehow, I think humming's just Mags's version of breathing. She literally never stops. My fingers pretend-snip nervously over a tangled strand of hair. My aunt's smile gathers into a careful purse.

"How about options, and you can choose? We could swing through town and get some burgers, or we could go home for supper. It's spaghetti and meatballs night, I think."

Spaghetti and meatballs night? I keep my eyes from bugging. That sounds *official*. Do Mags and Uncle Cameron have a kitchen staff in that giant house or something? I really have no idea what to expect of Windy Hall. The way my mom describes it, I half anticipate jeering concrete gargoyles and rusted iron gates, but sometimes Mom exaggerates when she's upset. For the first time in days, my stomach growls. "We can just go to the house, thanks. Spaghetti sounds all right."

27

"Spaghetti it is!" Mags waits a beat, then asks, "Your mom tell you much about me?"

"A little," I lie to be polite. Mom's never even mentioned Mags. She's always too busy tongue-lashing Uncle Cameron. Mom says he's the "kind" respectable folks oughtn't be caught dead around—brash, offbeat, embarrassing. *"Ran off to a fancy college and came back weird. Then he didn't have the sense to sell that old place after our folks died."* Mom's always been upset Uncle Cameron inherited Windy Hall, even though she would never live there. I squirm in my seat and scratch Bela's ear. Part of me is dying of curiosity to see what my uncle's like.

And even though I should be nervous about Windy Hall? The horror-loving ghoul in me is secretly straining to catch my first glimpse of Mom's nightmare fuel.

"We'll have to get to know each other, then," Mags says. Bela Pugosi stretches in my lap and starts sniffing the air vent. We must be getting close.

The sunset has painted the sky a vivid blue with bubblegum pink clouds as Mags turns down a long gravel road lined with pecan trees that break into a clearing. Bela's going nuts in my lap now, painting slimy trails across my window with his stubby little snoot.

My eyes bug out of my head and my jaw drops. Mags chuckles.

Looming in the distance is a massive hulk of a house, with a sprawling porch downstairs and upstairs, and more chimneys than any house has business having. Windy Hall is huge all right, but that's not why I'm gawking.

Every last board and brick of the colossal old mansion is painted a different brilliant hue of the rainbow, right down to the electric-purple-and-teal railing. A wide flounce of zinnias, sunflowers, and other plants I don't recognize encircle the porch like a dancer's skirt. There's a row of bikes, a van, and a couple of motorcycles parked in the driveway, but Mags rolls right by it, following a gravel road away from the house.

In the weedy lawn, a bonfire the size of a car is roaring, and a couple dozen people sit on lawn chairs and half-buried tires. They balance plates and drinks on their knees, laughing and waving at Mags as we drive by. Someone's playing a banjo, and a little kid runs around barefoot wearing a soccer jersey and a tutu.

In the dimming light, I see a massive, ambling garden to the left. Not the snooty "take a turn about the grounds with me, Mildred" kind of garden I've been picturing with hedgerows and sculptures. I'm talking dozens of cabbages, vast patches of pumpkins and tomatoes, wheelbarrows painted like ladybugs, scarecrows, curving wire tunnels covered in twisting vines, and a wooden cutout of a person bent over with floral bloomers showing. The whole rambling mess appears to be parsed out into little sections divided by makeshift fences of bamboo or colorful cinder blocks.

Mags parks the Jetta beside a chipped old toilet full of dirt and pansies. I drag myself out into the muggy twilight, knees wobbly. Bela Pugosi uses the bathroom in the grass as Mags gets my bag from the trunk. I squint, trying to make sense of it all. The bit of garden nearest to the car is a messy soup of black flowers, and for some reason, old porcelain doll heads and a sign that reads POISON. I shudder.

What have you gotten me into, Mom? I think. I feel mad at her for the first time. She had me expecting a snobby old house, lonely corridors, strict rules, dusty books—but this? I have no idea what to do here. If there are rules or expectations at all, I can't decipher them. This place is an alien planet.

"It's different than you expected?" Mags calls.

I nod.

"Let's eat, all right? Then I'll explain."

There's a long row of trailers with porch lights on. Mags leads me to the nearest one. Before we even get to the door, a balding man in a T-shirt opens it, waving us in.

So this is the brother Mom has such beef with. He looks *nothing* like her, with deeply tanned skin, a bold nose, and dark eyes. But he seems nice enough. His lined smile is mild and quiet, and his cheeks and bifocals are smudged with baking flour. The smell of warm vanilla drifts through the door.

Showtime. My spine stretches, I wipe my feet politely on the mat, and I stop picking at my fingers. Mom needs as many folks vouching for her as we can get, and that means mending fences with her estranged brother. I stick out my hand. "Uncle Cameron?"

The man raises a bushy gray eyebrow. He and Aunt Mags exchange a *look.*

"Oh dear," says Aunt Mags finally. "Your mom really didn't tell you anything at all about me, did she? Cameron is the name my family called *me* as a child. But Cameron isn't my name, and I'm not your uncle. I'm your *auntie,* your mother's *sister,*" Mags says, emphasizing the words patiently, like she's done it a hundred times. "I'd love it if you'd just call me Mags."

I hesitate a second, processing. Oh. Mags is trans. I've

heard of trans people in school, but I've never met one until today. *That makes so much more sense*, I think. *I look related to Mags, even.* I bob my head to show I understand.

The man beside Mags gives me a kind smile, and I realize my face has probably been doing thinking gymnastics. Mags pats the man on the shoulder affectionately and says, "You do have an uncle, at any rate. This is my dear husband, Luca. He makes beautiful sugar cookies, and if my nose doesn't deceive me, they're already out of the oven."

I smile and let Mags and Luca escort me inside.

But my thoughts are whirring, and it's making my belly feel full of minnows. *Why didn't Mom tell me about Aunt Mags? Is it her dislike of change, like when she calls me Magnolia Grace instead of Sparrow?* I feel another surge of irritation toward my mom. Then I immediately feel awful, because who knows why Mom does anything she does. It almost always comes back to her sad shadow, so I let it go.

I follow Mags and Luca through the cozy living room. Mags points to doors down the little hallway. "The first is the bathroom, and the one beside it is your room. Wash up, and I'll scoot down to the big house and bring back spaghetti."

I don't ask why Mags and Luca live here instead of at Windy Hall. Or why dinner seems to happen there instead of here. Or why the grounds are absolutely swarming with people. I just stumble into the bathroom, nerves raw and exhausted.

I scrub, then dry my hands on the ragged hand towel. Just as I reach to turn off the bathroom light, the hairs on my arms and neck raise, like a forest creature fluffing itself trying to seem bigger. I let a trembling hand fall away from the light switch. Out of the corner of my eye, my reflection in the mirror seems . . . different.

I feel like something's there, waiting for me to look. And that should scare me, but instead my chest fills with a bittersweet ache I can't quite name.

I swivel toward my old nemesis—my reflection—heart fluttering. For that split second, part of me hopes I'll see something new. Maybe even some*one* new. A happier me. But all I see in the glass is a travel-worn girl, looking more out of place than ever. Because, of course. *What's wrong with me tonight?*

It's been a very long day, I reason. A long week, even, and I've been thrown enough curveballs to make anyone feel off their game. Still, I keep snatching glances at my reflection as I cup cold water from the faucet over my mouth and chin, washing off beads of sweat.

As I inch the door open and turn off the light, Mom's slurring rants about her childhood home replay in my ears: *You couldn't pay me enough money to go back to Windy Hall. That place plays tricks on your mind, and you can feel its hatefulness creeping from every floorboard, stream, and stone. Don't you ever go there, Magnolia Grace.*

But I'm Sparrow. And, thanks to Mom, Windy Hall is exactly where I've ended up. Her rants don't usually scare me, but I promise myself I'll be careful if I notice myself having any more odd feelings.

I take a deep, shuddering breath and hurry toward the glowing kitchen. As I sit down in front of a plate of steaming spaghetti, I make a mental note to ask Aunt Mags for a night-light before I go to bed.

Chapter Four
Sparrow Imagining Things

Sparrow Malone

Mr. Brewster

Science Homework, Sixth Grade

Animal Habitat Essay

Tardigrades, or water bears as some people call them, are microscopic, eight-legged animals. Their name means "slow stepper," because of the ambling way their tiny legs move. But what they lack in speed they make up for in survival skill. They've been found alive in the harshest deserts, the darkest ocean trenches, the frozen Antarctic, and in the lonely vacuum of space. They can even survive deadly radiation and geometry class!

This ability to survive comes from their unique cells, which can survive desiccation (the process of drying out completely). Scientists study water bears in harsh conditions to test the limits of their endurance and learn their secrets. But surviving and thriving are two different things, in my opinion. Tardigrades seem at their happiest and healthiest on moist moss and lichen, and other places where water is plentiful.

I wake entangled in a strange bedspread and sweaty hair, heart pounding like I've run a race in my sleep. For several panicked breaths, I can't move. *Sleep paralysis*, it's called. This happens to me sometimes. I can't remember where or who I am. Only one coherent thought rolls through my brain, and I clamp on to it like a drowning swimmer: *Mom!* The gut knowledge that she's missing, far away, freaks me out. I need to find her. My fingers twitch first, then my toes, and finally my limbs rev to life.

In a valiant attempt to stand, my foot gets tangled in the sheet and I tumble to the floor and land with a graceless *oomf.* The floor sounds hollow, which is odd. My collision reverberates through the room, and the windows above tremble in their panes.

My sore ribs squeeze out a long groan as my mind clears. *I'm at Mags's trailer at Windy Hall,* I remember. *Mom's not here. She's in rehab.* I spit carpet fuzz from my mouth and nod to myself like this is normal information and not the end of the world.

"I'm okay, I'm okay, I'm okay . . ." I mutter.

The corners of my eyes prickle, and I try to resist the instinct to crawl back into bed and curl up like a threatened pill bug. Because it finally sinks in: Mom's fallen apart. *Okay. It happens,* I tell myself. She's messed up before. Not usually in such a spectacular way, and not where other people can see it. And we've never been separated. But still—I know what comes next in the phoenix cycle of Mom: Sparrow keeps it together, Sparrow learns the rules of Windy Hall, and then Sparrow impresses everybody until they tell Mom what an amazing parent she is, and she recovers. It'll be fine.

First, I'll learn the rules of fitting in here—at Windy Hall, then at Brightbarrel Middle. If moving towns constantly has taught me anything, it's that every place has its own distinct *folkways* (a word I picked up from a waiting-room magazine). It means: a set of shared values unique to an area or region, like whether you put sugar in your corn bread, call people sir and ma'am, or wave hi to strangers on the sidewalk. Get the folkways right, and you can charm anyone. Get a few wrong, though, and suddenly everyone's whispering behind your back, or worse, you become invisible.

"Like any good scientist, Sparrow must observe and learn," I narrate under my breath, soft enough that Mags and Luca won't hear through the door. "After that, our intrepid explorer can make a good impression and get things back on track."

I crack the bedroom door and glance downward. Sure enough, my Wolverine sweatshirt and denim shorts wait on the floor just outside, freshly washed and folded . . . with Bela Pugosi curled atop them, wheezing in his sleep. Since that first day Mags showed up, she's washed this outfit every night, so I keep wearing it until I have to go back to school.

I coax Bela off by scratching his ears, then snatch my clothes and tiptoe into the bathroom to change. Bela wants to follow me in, and I let him. I'm pretty sure the weird reflection in the bathroom mirror last night was me hallucinating from exhaustion. But that didn't stop me from throwing a towel over the glass when I got up for a midnight pee. I'll need the mirror to get ready, and having Bela with me feels safer. If a monster snatches me, at least there will be a slobbery witness.

I yank the sweatshirt over my head. It smells like Mags's lavender fabric softener and also a little like Bela's flea shampoo, but it's kind of nice. I frown as I notice a pinprick hole forming at the sleeve and try not to think about how scrambled my body will feel once my safe outfit falls apart.

Today, we're both holding together.

Now for this *hair*. I tug the towel off the mirror and wince. For the past few days, I haven't been able to deal with combing it—just rearranging it into a knot on top of my head, adding a new elastic, and hoping for the best. But last night's bad sleep transformed it into an overpowered Tangela Pokémon, and I can't even find the elastics inside the snarls. I'll be introduced to new people today—Mags is taking me to meet-and-greet teachers this afternoon before I start school tomorrow. So I have to tackle it, overwhelmed or not.

I forgot my brush at home, and my stomach sours as my fingers walk over the knots, trying to find a place to start. It's never been this bad before, and it's bothering me that I can't do my usual imaginary haircut routine right away.

Besides, I want out of this weird bathroom as fast as possible. I start with an auburn snarl and *pull*, but the strands don't give. *Ouch, ouch, flippin' OUCH.*

My chest tightens, and thoughts leapfrog one another in a disorganized rush. *I have to fix this. I hate messing with my stupid hair. This would be so much easier at home. I wish I could just buzz it all off.* This last thought makes my heart go jumpy. God, Mom would be so mad if I ever did that. She freaks out even when I just want to trim a few inches. What's wrong with me today?

I feel trapped, like the time when I was four and my foot got stuck in the rails of the chair in our rental apartment. I'd been convinced medics would come and amputate my foot to save the chair—it never occurred to me they'd cut apart the chair, not *me*. Mom finally got my ankle out using cooking spray, and I'd cried for an hour after. But I'm *twelve* now, not four, and I shouldn't be melting down like this.

My flushed face gathers, and tears collect in my throat. In my head, I picture screaming or kicking the cabinets in frustration, though I won't, *obviously*. But I can't go out like this, and I can't stay in the bathroom forever or Mags and Luca will start wondering . . .

Tap, tap, tap. "Sparrow, do you have everything you

need?" Mags sounds breezy and chipper, a morning fanatic through and through. My thoughts stop spinning, frozen by the distraction.

I pause, staring at the impossible knots in the mirror, considering Mags's question. What would *help* this mess? A Weedwacker? A cranial transplant?

"My hair's . . . being a little stubborn," I call, trying to sound fine. "Mom usually does it."

Mags's muffled "I see" comes through the door, and I congratulate myself for my impromptu lie. Mom hasn't touched my hair in years, but now Mags will think I'm pitiful because I need Mom, instead of seeming just plain . . . pitiful.

"Come out to the kitchen, and I'll try my hand at sorting it, if you like! Luca's made waffles."

I unlock the door and open it sheepishly. My aunt looks nice—yesterday's butterfly hair clips are swapped out for a floral handkerchief that coordinates with purple overalls. Just for second, I'm glad Mom isn't here to comment—she thinks overalls are "tacky." But on Mags, I think they're cute, in an older-person sort of way. Her thin brows twitch upward as she glances at my hair, but if she regrets volunteering to detangle the mess, she hides it.

"If you like strawberries, you're in luck," Mags confides, waving me out. "One of our neighbors just brought a pint, straight from the field. Sunshine in your mouth!"

I pad meekly in the wake of her grapefruit perfume all the way to a table that's already set with plates and napkins in the tiny dining room. Luca whistles in the kitchen close by, trilling like a wood thrush as steam rises from his waffle iron. He gives me a shy wave. "Morning!"

I mirror his wave and echo, "Good morning." I settle in a chair and fork a waffle onto my plate, but my arms and knees won't stop trembling. I'm pretty sure Mags notices.

She pours some orange juice and slides the glass in front of me. "Drink this. You didn't eat much yesterday, kiddo."

Fair point. I sip, then gulp. I'm not crazy about the concerned wrinkle on Mags's forehead as she watches me, because I need her to know I'm usually way more mature and confident than this. "Just nervous energy," I say, shrugging. "I'm excited to meet my new teachers and check out the gardens."

"Mmmmm. There are a few kids your age you might get along with here, too," Mags offers between sips of coffee. "But we've got plenty of time for all that. Eat some waffles, have some eggs. You've had a lot of change. It's good to be nice to your body when it's adjusting to a different place."

I want to argue that I'm a pro at adapting to new environments, but I'm not sure how to word it without making us seem flaky for moving so often. So I eat a perfect square of waffle instead, chewing slowly, then dab my lips with a napkin. Perfect manners—Mom would be proud. A clump of snarled hair swings over my face, somewhat ruining the effect.

"I have just the thing for that," Mags announces. She sails out of the room, leaving Luca whistling over the sink and me wolfing down food now that no one's watching. By the time Mags returns with a sophisticated-looking hairbrush, my plate is bare.

I scoot to the back of my chair to make it easier for Mags to reach Mt. Bird's Nest. Her soft hands are so skilled, I barely notice she's started on the tangles before she drops one of the hair elastics onto the table.

"So, since your mom hasn't talked much about me or Windy Hall, have you got any burning questions?"

Oh, Mom's said plenty about Windy Hall, I think. But Mags is right; Mom avoided concrete specifics. My pulse quickens. It seems like cheating, somehow, to finally get detailed answers—it's basically a betrayal of one of Mom's many unspoken rules. *We don't ask questions about Windy Hall.* I start with something safe. "How come you and Luca live in this trailer instead of the big house?"

Mags sighs softly. "Oh, you know how it is with memories and places sometimes."

I really don't, but I nod anyway.

"Some days I spent in that house aren't nice to remember again and again, but it brings me joy to share the space with people. It's so big, I split it up into apartments."

"So . . . you're a landlady?"

"Hmm? Oh goodness, no. The house is just for friends who need a place for a while. There's a young couple from the college where I teach—they're interning with one of the master gardeners here at Windy Hall. And other college students earning this or that horticultural and botany degree, who use the garden for their projects."

"People can earn grades from pulling *weeds*?"

Mags chuckles, and the flexible brush glides over the left side of my head easily, sending nice shivers down my arms. "There's more to it than that. But yes, more or less."

I wait a beat, thinking. "Are your bad memories of Windy Hall the same as my mom's?"

The brush pauses mid-snarl. Mags lets out a long sigh, and I wonder if I've pushed too hard. *Ugh, Sparrow, now she's upset.* But then Mags speaks, her voice thoughtful.

"People can have different experiences of the same things, so I can't speak for your mother's feelings. Partly because it's her story to tell from her own perspective. And partly because I wasn't around for all of it, though I wish I could have been. But suffice it to say, my parents weren't gentle people. They didn't understand anyone different from them, and their ability to offer love and support was limited by their poor view of me, through no fault of my own. Does that make sense?"

This wasn't the answer I expected. My insides suddenly feel like a jumbled suitcase. Not only do I not understand half of what my aunt just said, but Mags also didn't talk about having shadows, like Mom does, and doesn't seem to blame the house itself for being evil. So I twist in my chair and ask her outright. "But do you think Mom might hate Windy Hall because . . . because it's, like . . . possessed or something?"

Mags cackles so hard, her bosom bounces and her face becomes a topographic map of laugh lines. My neck warms, and I spin back around in my seat and clamp my mouth tight. Luca swivels at the sink and clucks his tongue at Mags, muttering something in Italian and waggling a drying towel in admonishment. Mags glides her fingers through my hair, now long and smooth, and my fingers immediately move up to *snip, snip, snip* it.

"Forgive me, Sparrow. Luca is correct. You asked an earnest question, and it deserves a serious answer. I assure you that, to my knowledge, Windy Hall is not possessed of any foul spirits. The most you have to worry about here is ticks and the occasional pumpkin guts battle."

"Pumpkin guts?"

"Oh, you'll see. And now, I have a question for *you.*"

Here we go again. For the past few days, I've answered so many questions from my principal and teachers, and then even more from a nice-enough social worker. How often do I eat? How much time do I spend at home alone? Do I ever feel afraid of my mom? When's the last time I went to the dentist?

Automatically, my arms snake around each other in front of my chest, giving me armor and a little safe space to think. I expect Mags to ask about Mom, about my feelings, about why I keep wearing the same clothes over and over. She's probably thinking Mom doesn't do a good job of shopping for me or something, which is totally unfair. I'm ready to explain I have other outfits—I just *feel* right in this one—when Mags surprises me.

"I need to run an errand. Your auntie's getting older, so I'm trading last year's slacks for something better suited to these cute new curves. Would you mind keeping me and Bela company? I'm thinking we'll go meet your teachers after, then ice cream to celebrate." Mags stands and strikes a dramatic pose, like she's one of those fluffy-robed actors in old black-and-white movies. "Give 'em the ol' razzle-dazzle!"

My arms drop in relief, and I giggle. *Oh thank god.* Saying yes to easy requests is my jam. If Mags is happy, I'm one step closer to being back on track. Learn the ropes, study the environment, and then, like Mags said, give everyone *the ol' razzle-dazzle.*

Soon, we're bumping along in the Jetta, Bela drawing cryptic doggie sigils on the glass with his nose, until we arrive at what looks like a thrift shop in an old strip mall with a sign that screams TRADER JOLENE'S in neon letters.

Inside, Mags chats with someone at the register, and I

wander off once she gives me the okay. I beeline straight to the bookshelves. I find nature books about mycology (the study of mushrooms), entomology (the study of insects), and one about deep-sea exploration. The covers are pretty, if a little worn. That's okay—that way, the pages are broken in, staying open wherever I'm reading. Thumbing through chapters, I smile to see some facts I don't already know. Definite keepers. I flip the books over for price stickers, but there are none.

Just as I consider finding Mags for help, I smell my aunt's perfume nearby. She pokes her head around the bookshelf and grins over a pile of glittery fabric. "I've decided my new favorite dress color is *sparkles*," she declares.

"Sweet! Sparkles suit you." They really do, too—I'm not just being nice. Little shimmers of light dance off the blouses, and the glimmering matches my aunt's eyes.

"How about you—find anything spiffy?"

I nod. "I have a few dollars, too, but I can't find price stickers."

"Oh, it's just the honor system here—take what you need, bring what you can. The books are yours, if you like. And anything else in the store that suits your fancy, too! I'll be in the dressing room."

I hug the books to myself and gaze around. Clothes shopping makes me want to crawl right out of my skin, but I didn't want to tell my aunt that. I skirt around the wide array of patterns in the girls and ladies' section, feeling a little queasy. In the animal world, when a creature is hunting for a meal inside a large flock or school, it becomes overwhelmed with something called the confusion effect—so much movement and so many options make the predator's brain short-circuit, and it can't lock on to a single target. This is how I feel now, staring over this sea of pinks, ruffles, and elaborate straps. I try imagining these shirts or dresses on my body, and my palms start to sweat.

There's a reason I wear Mom's hand-me-downs, and it's not just because money's tight. I hate even thinking about clothes. Hate choosing, hate looking at them, and hate how everything feels wrong.

Nope. I swivel on my heel and head back toward the bookshelves, when, out of the corner of my eye, I see a flash of red that practically screams, *"Hey, you with the crush on the nature books, LOOK HERE."* My feet squeak to a stop on the tile.

It's a pair of red boots. They're not orange-red like rusted hinges or Georgia clay. They're *red*-red like *Amanita muscaria*—toadstool mushrooms, match heads, or blood. They look newish, so I give them an experimental sniff. The sweet-and-smoky smell of the leather makes me dizzy, but in a good way, like when you inhale peppermint tea after a long day. The thick rubber soles prove sturdy and flexible. I suspect they make a gorgeous, satisfying clomp when you walk in them. I picture myself striding alone down the covered sidewalk at my old school, and the ecstasy in my soul is impossible to cram into tiny words. Basically? I'm in love.

I glance up at the sign taped to the shoe rack. MENS SIZE 6/LADIES SIZE 8, it reads. Mom's too-tight shoes are sevens, which means these will probably fit me, right?

I pause, already crouched on the floor, socked foot poised to plunge into the left boot. I gnaw a hole in my lip. Mom would hate what I'm doing. In my head, I see her mouth turn into that scared, pinched line as her eyes dart around, worrying someone is watching. *"Those look so mannish, Maggie Grace. Don't you want something nice? Something pretty? Not some old work boots."*

But Mom's not here. She's gone. I hear Mags calling my name and footsteps walking up behind me. In that split second, I make a deal with myself. If I don't cry, I can have the boots, if they fit. Mom would hate them, but that's fine—I can wear these outrageously gorgeous clodhopper boots, just as a treat while she's not around. And then . . .

Then, I'll go be awesome. I'll make top grades and win over my new teachers. And everything will be fine again.

I slide my feet into the boots: a perfect fit. If my heart could throw confetti, we'd need a serious vacuum cleaner.

"Ohhh, bold choice!" Mags says as she approaches, clapping her hands. "Comfortable. Nice color!"

I blush and tromp to the mirror, curious to see how I look. *Oh wow.* Something squirms inside my chest. I clap my hand over my mouth as I smile like a maniac. I feel . . . what's the word? I can't describe it. The sensation is electric and foreign, but not bad. It's a mixture of excitement, pride, and fear, like the first time I jumped off a high-dive board. The boots look brave and sturdy—like a little piece of inside-Sparrow has found its way onto my feet.

"What do you think? Keepers, or should we keep looking?" asks Mags.

"I think . . . I'm never taking them off," I murmur, twisting my right foot to admire the heel. Just then, the sun emerges from behind a cloud outside. Harsh noon light spills in from the shop-front windows, making the colored flyers taped to them glow like stained glass. Jerking my head away from the brightness, I catch sight of a shadow unfurling onto the tiled floor. It starts at the soles of my new boots, then trails off behind me: a Sparrow-shaped puddle expanding like newly spilled ink. *Weird.* It's larger than life, and I imagine I see the fingers waggle a hello at me—something my hands are definitely not doing. Its head tweaks just one inquisitive inch to the side.

Aren't you going to wave back? it seems to ask.

A shadow. Like Mom's? My heart halts a beat. No. *This isn't real.* Because I, Sparrow, am a rational person who understands the difference between a metaphor and reality. Mom's shadow—no matter how she talks about it, is just her soft way of explaining her addiction. My throat tightens as I realize this is the first time I've thought *that* word in my head about Mom. Mom . . . has an addiction. The shadow's still looking back at me, head slightly off from where it ought to be.

Whatever this is—probably a bend in the shop window glass refracting light in a funky way—it's an illusion. And I won't let my imagination hijack my awesome boots moment. I made a deal with myself, and that's what I'm focusing on: I get these gorgeous red clodhoppers, and Brightbarrel Middle gets the best student to ever stomp through its hallways. And soon, Mom and I get our lives back. I refuse to lose it.

"You ready to go meet your teachers?" Mags asks.

I nod, turning to follow. "Teachers, then ice cream?"

"Teachers, then ice cream."

Chapter Five

Sparrow Definitely Losing It

Sparrow Malone

Ms. Ishihara

Science Homework, Fifth Grade

Report on Megafauna

The word "*megafauna*" means "giant animals." Megafauna are creatures weighing more than ninety-nine pounds as adults. Today, this includes bears, elephants, moose, and bison.

But around 12,000 years ago, there were dozens of genera of megafauna in North America that no longer exist. Woolly mammoths are the most famous, but there were also 3,500-pound bison, armadillo-like animals called glyptodons that were the size of small cars, and giant beavers as big as today's black bears!

Some scientists think these animals disappeared due to drastic climate change. Others believe prehistoric humans are to blame—that we hunted megafauna to extinction. I hypothesize that a combination of these factors caused the extinctions. Whatever the reason, the world became a less friendly place for their enormous lives, and they disappeared. It's nice, though, that smaller versions of their kind survived, and their family lives on through adaptation.

For some reason, I expected Brightbarrel Middle to have a covered walkway just like my last school, which is silly. Every school is different. Still, I'm panicking without my sidewalk ritual.

Plus? It's weird without Mom here. When she's anxious, I'm the brave one, and my own fears stay buried. Now that she's gone, my insecurities surface like poisonous cane toads in a pond, and it's tough to find my game-face groove. *What if everyone's smarter than me? Oh god, why didn't I change out of my safe outfit before we came?*

I flex my feet inside my new boots. I need to pull an Uno Reverse card on my nerves. *I'm not scared*, I think. *I'm just excited.*

"Ready, Sparrow?" Mags asks. She's plopped Bela into her sturdy purse—bringing him with us on the school tour, apparently.

"Ready."

We walk through the front entrance into the breezeway, where Mags waves through the glass wall to the lady at the front-office desk. The woman smiles and presses a button, unlocking the doors for us. A blast of air-conditioning whooshes around my legs, making my fine leg hairs stand on end.

Mags chats with the front desk lady, who hands me a class schedule with a school map and welcomes me to Brightbarrel.

I breathe a grateful sigh when I see the classrooms are attached to a gigantic square circuit of hallway around the perimeter of the building—no chance of getting lost during my first week. In the center of the school is the library and gym, which seems to double as the cafeteria. One less thing to worry about! I grin and make a kissy face at Bela, who grunts in excitement.

The first class is geometry, and a young-looking teacher with a mullet and a bow tie greets Mags and me quietly in the back of the class while the students take a test. "Hello! I'm Teacher Jones! I'm so excited to have you in our class, Sparrow."

My heart hops at the sound of my name—I didn't even have to correct it from the dreaded Magnolia Grace. How? Aunt Mags, maybe? "Thanks!" I throw back my shoulders, smiling. "I really love math," I lie. My ears flame, ashamed of me for being such a bootlick. The teacher beams.

"Hey, that's what I like to hear! Our class is a little ahead of the program already, but we'll get you caught up, no problem. Your aunt tells me you've been through a lot lately, so let's not focus on grades for the time being."

Caught up? I eyeball the test paper on the student's desk nearest to me—it's solving complementary angles, a chapter I tackled at the end of last year. I drum an impatient rhythm with my toes inside my new boots. I'm annoyed I can't grab a pencil and prove myself. *Don't pity me!* I want to blurt, but I bite my tongue.

Meanwhile, the girl at the desk is doodling angry tornadoes in the answer blanks. She must feel me staring, because she tosses her wavy hair and shoots icicles from her deep brown eyes. Desk Girl is wearing an elegant linen sundress that fits just so, and a dainty gold necklace with the letter K dangling from it. It's the sort of getup Mom always wishes she could afford to buy me (and I'm secretly happy she can't). Desk Girl looks at home in these clothes. And, honest to goodness, my knees buckle a little, she's so pretty. I'm not supposed to notice this—another unofficial Malone family rule: *You can't get crushes on girls. People won't understand, Magnolia.* But a clumsy squeak escapes my throat anyway.

The girl raises an eyebrow like I just ate gum off the floor. It occurs to me that a well-adjusted person would try to make friends with her. I glance around. Mags and Teacher Jones are still deep in hushed conversation. The girl stares, arms crossed, waiting for me to say something. She's edgy from bombing her test, I guess. My mind flits to a book I read once about bowerbirds, who bring shiny objects to the girls they want to impress. Impulsively, I whisper to the girl, "Seventy-four degrees."

Desk Girl scowls. "Are you supposed to be the weatherman?"

"No, um, it's the answer to the question? Angle PQR is

seventy-four degrees." My stomach protests. Usually I don't help people cheat, but making friends is on my to-do list. And math answers are the shiniest token I have to offer this girl on the fly, even if it makes me feel sketchy.

Desk Girl pulls a comical face and nods in approval like *I'm* the one taking a test, and I just passed. Warmth floods me, and I smile as she erases her scribble and jots down the answer. "Hi, new kid. I'm Kylie."

Mission accomplished. Before I can introduce myself, Mags taps my elbow and we're off to the next class. I repeat Kylie's name in my head a few times, memorizing it.

Second period is language arts, then computer for third period, and science for fourth. Mostly, Mags and I just stick our heads in for a few seconds, the teachers introduce themselves, and we hurry on to the next class.

As we head to science, I'm trying to seem sweet and rule-abiding. But when I peep at my shadow on the long stretch of wall, it's strutting with its hands in its pockets. I blink, not trusting my eyeballs. My shadow is doing my secret covered-sidewalk swagger!

I curl my shoulders forward and clasp my hands in front of me. But out of the corner of my eye, I swear I can still see myself parading like a rooster.

What is *happening*? Am I hallucinating? Should I tell someone? My belly clenches as I remember the weird mirror reflection my first night in the trailer, and Mags's reassurance that Windy Hall isn't somehow cursed.

Get a grip, *Sparrow*, I tell myself. This is my only shot at first impressions. And after my meltdown over my hair this morning, I don't want to worry my aunt. How would that reflect on Mom? My pulse quickens. *The shadow is just stress*, I repeat. I swallow hard and check the map on the class schedule.

"Here we go. Science, Room 402," I croak. I ignore the dark shape on the floor as it slithers through the door beneath my feet, wriggling jazz hands at me.

Mags smiles and introduces us. Immediately, I'm drowning in an armful of lists and homework sheets. Mr. Fullilove, the teacher, informs me through his walrus mustache that I'll be expected to catch up on several weeks' worth of homework for the class unit study on food and agriculture. "Since your grade at your last school was already low, it's important you dedicate some effort, Miss Malone."

I'm stunned. Why does he think my grade was low? It was an A. He assumes I wasn't putting in *effort*? I grind my teeth. My science grade was the next-to-highest in the class!

But I never argue with teachers. Behind Mr. Fullilove—who is definitely *not* full-of-love, I decide—my shadow spreads across the wall until it towers with heaving shoulders. It sprouts two white eyes that glow like looming headlights. *Not real*, I think. *Focus on the botched grade.* I glance pitifully up at Mags, but I'm not sure how to ask for help.

When Mr. Fullilove turns to grab another folder, Mags leans close. "Everything all right, kiddo? You're looking green."

"I think they got my transcript wrong," I whisper. "My grade should be a ninety-nine."

"Do you want me to call your old school and straighten things out?" Mags asks. "I don't mind at all."

I shake my head. I need a clean start, and I don't want any more questions about Mom or weird attention.

Mr. Fullilove is back with more papers, and my shadow flexes enormous muscles, then pretends to bonk the teacher on the head with a comically large hammer from behind. "Now, you'll need to have this all finished by the end of the semester, plus your current assignments . . ."

"*Roger*," Mags says politely. "Considering Sparrow's current circumstances—"

I flinch at *circumstances* but listen as Mags continues.

"—might we consider a substantial extra credit project that fulfills this unit's objectives? Say, a cultivation activity at the community garden, overseen by one of the botany students there, plus a paper discussing the main points on the assigned reading?"

Mr. Fullilove chews the inside of his mouth for a moment, then nods. "I suppose that would fulfill the learning requirements, yes. And considering your niece's unique situation, I think we can allow it. I'll send an email with specific instructions to your student account. See you in class tomorrow, Miss Malone!"

As we make our way to my final classroom, I look back to see the shadow shrink and glide along behind me, docile as any pet. The glowing eyes stay trained on my face, and I shiver. Mags catches me looking backward but doesn't seem to see what's following me. She pats my shoulder.

"Oh, don't worry about Mr. Fullilove, doll. I've known him a good long time. He's a serious soul but only in his appreciation for structure. If you're honest with him, I believe you'll find him sympathetic."

I nod, throat dry. I don't look back again.

"Last class!" my aunt chirps. I glance down at the now-wrinkled schedule. My palms go clammy. The only elective with an open spot is drama. This is good, because Mom always goes starry-eyed whenever she asks about play auditions. She'd be so excited if I even tried out, which would go a long way in raising her spirits.

But it's bad, too, since the very thought of performing onstage makes acid creep up my throat.

Mags and I enter the drama room, which is my smallest class by far—maybe half as many students as my nonelectives. Ten, maybe twelve kids are sprawled across faded rugs in front of long bookshelves, each one with a novel in hand. A few are reading aloud to a partner in hushed, animated voices.

"Hello, hello, hello!" calls a man in a short ponytail and a goatee as he jogs over. He's got a soft Tennessee accent and talks very fast. "You must be Sparrow Malone! I'm Mr. Fitz, and I'm very thrilled to be your drama teacher this semester."

I try hard to mirror Mr. Fitz's enthusiasm—not an easy task. I force a whoosh of cheery energy through me, like I'm one of those dancing used-car-lot inflatables. "It's great to meet you! So, are y'all doing a play this year?"

"Not till next unit, three weeks from now. I like to lay a good groundwork of emotion identification study before we try to bring those feelings to the stage. And since I also teach creative writing part-time at the community college, we'll do some exploratory composition during the next couple of weeks."

My heart soars. *Writing.* It's not a lead role in a play yet, but a fatter writing binder full of As would be the next-best thing to show Mom when I finally get to visit her.

"That sounds awesome, Mr. Fitz. I can't wait!" My voice starts strong, then cracks as I spot my shadow. It's not tethered to me anymore. It's crawling Spidey-style up the poster-covered wall across the room, above the long bookcases.

"Well, since we've just started class, you're welcome to join us!" Mr. Fitz says, gesturing to the reading area. "We're picking out books in groups of two or three, and seeing if we can identify the emotions of the characters in the dialogue."

I can tell Mr. Fitz hopes I'll say yes. And I want to. But I've frozen in place, staring just behind Mr. Fitz. My shadow peels itself away from the wall. The me-shaped pool of darkness grows, filling out as it stretches from flat to three-dimensional. My pulse races as it drops to the floor suddenly and crawls toward me on fingers and tiptoes like a determined palmetto bug, white-orb eyes glowing. Shadow weaves around oblivious students on the carpet and halts just beside my teacher. It cocks its head this way and that. It waits. *Your move.*

Blood pounds in my ears, and my hands and feet go cold. *What do I do?* No one else can see it. *Maybe if I ignore this . . . this hallucination, it'll go away*, I think.

Aunt Mags mistakes my silence as indecision. "Up to you, hon! You can stay for last period if you like! Bela and I are content to run an errand or two."

I nod stupidly. Mags smiles and waves bye. I follow the drama teacher toward the bookshelves, and my shadow skitters alongside him, waving for me to follow. The room starts to tilt-a-whirl around me, and even though Mr. Fitz talks loudly, it's like my brain lags. His words come to me in a jumble, and I have to repeat the sounds over and over in my head until they start to make sense. I'm losing my game face and falling down, down, down into anxiety.

Hello, sweat. It's been a while since I felt this nervous in school. What did Mr. Fitz just say? He's pointing to a couple of kids just by the bookshelf. I force myself to really focus so I can hear his words. "Sully and Wynn, this is Sparrow. She'll be in your group today."

The preoccupied kids nod vaguely and keep talking.

"It's good to have you here, Sparrow!" my teacher says, then abandons me.

I try to call out "thanks, Mr. Fitz," but the words come out in jumbled nonsense: "Tanks fizzer mish." My face flames, and I steal a glance to see if my group members heard my anxious babble.

To my relief, they don't even notice me. They're arguing over which book to read from, and I'm too self-conscious to interrupt them.

One—Wynn, I think—is a round, sunburned white girl with choppy green hair and one of the wildest outfits I've ever seen. She's wearing a pink Hawaiian shirt, fishing shorts to the knee, and net-pattern tights underneath—with shimmery, silver rubber sardines stuck every which way inside them. She argues with Sully, but the ease of their bickering makes me think they're friends, or maybe even family.

"You've read *Holes* a billion times, my dude!"

"Yes, because it's an excellent book."

"I know, but you have it basically memorized! That's almost like cheating."

Sully sighs deeply and rolls his eyes, grazing long brown fingers over his peach-dyed twists. He's pretending he's had it with Wynn's attitude, but I can tell by his wry smirk and the way his shoulders stay relaxed that this is a game they play. He leans down and thumps the cover of the book Wynn's gripping with his knuckle. "Fine. But that short poetry book isn't dialogue, Wynn."

"This short poetry book is crammed with a thousand subtle *feelings*, Sully."

"It's not the only short thing crammed with feelings," Sully teases gently, dodging a playful swat from Wynn.

My shadow hovers between them, motioning me to join. I should, but I'm not sure what's more horrifying: The thought of approaching strangers while tongue-tied? Or stepping even an inch closer to that uncanny shadow version of myself?

Shadow throws its arms in the air, like I'm a hopeless cause. Then, it whirls toward the bookshelf, catlike. It bends and walks its fingers across a row of book spines, pausing on an old favorite of mine, *Doll Bones*.

Ehh? It gestures. *Come take it!*

I shake my head. Sorry, imaginary shadow. I'm frozen to this spot on the floor. This is my home now. Even though Mom needs me to excel in this class, my chicken legs won't cooperate, and I've lost my unstoppable nerve.

The white-orb eyes blink.

Then, Shadow shrugs and kneels at the corner of the rug where Sully and Wynn stand. My stomach lurches as the edge of the carpet actually lifts an inch or two in the shadow's fingers. Shadow blinks again.

"Oh, don't you dare," I wheeze.

Shadow moves to yank the rug, hard. "Okay, seriously, stop! Just stop! I'll go get the book!" I hiss the words at Shadow a little louder than I mean to.

The shadow lets go. I narrow my eyes at it, and it has the nerve to give me finger guns.

Oh, very nice. Evil *and* corny. I roll my eyes. In response, the shadow points at Sully and Wynn. My scowl freezes and slides right off my face.

Wynn and Sully aren't arguing anymore. They're too busy staring at me. I replay what I just said out loud and suppress a groan. *These two think I just volunteered to settle their banter over the book assignment,* I realize. Sully is suddenly quieter, but Wynn's passionate energy stays at full throttle.

"PLEASE DO," Wynn exclaims, clasping her hands and stepping closer. Earrings made from actual Goldfish crackers dangle from her pink earlobes, sealed with some sort of shiny-looking paint or glue. "Sully and I won't ever agree, so you'd be doing us a giant favor. I'm Wynn, by the way."

I pause a millisecond. Neither Wynn nor Sully look mad, just a little entertained by my outburst. And weirdly? This has a soothing effect. If they like boldness, I'll just roll with it.

"Okay," I say, skirting around my creepy shadow on my way to the bookshelf.

I pluck out *Doll Bones* and hand it to Wynn. "It was one of my favorites a couple years ago. Still is, I guess. It's about a haunted porcelain doll, and a group of friends who are growing apart. Lots of dialogue. Lots of feels."

"Perfect!" Wynn's face lights up as she thumbs through, and Sully nods in approval.

My shadow leans back on its elbows, like, *See? Told ya it was a good idea.*

Now that I'm officially part of the group of three, we spend the next half hour listening to Wynn read dialogue. Sully and I take turns picking words from a chart of emotions that describe how the character is likely feeling. I'm basically a pro at this; a lifetime of staying ahead of Mom's shifting moods has made me an expert at body language. A few times, Wynn insists on rereading the dialogue, adding more of the emotion we identified. She's good at it, too.

Wynn will be competition for a lead role, I think to myself.

If Mom's stuck in rehab long enough for me to audition for this year's play, I'll have to seriously practice in front of the mirror.

"Okay, gang!" Mr. Fitz calls, clapping his hands. "Eyes on me!"

Giggles and chatter fizzle as the room turns to the teacher. My eyes scan for the shadow, and I see it's curled up on the floor almost touching me, napping like a cat. I shudder and try to pay attention to Mr. Fitz.

"This unit's big project will be completed in groups, with the same folks you worked with today."

Wynn and Sully poke each other, then mime cheering in my direction. I feel my face flush, pleased. It's a good team. Sully's really smart, and Wynn's an incredible actress. I give them a thumbs-up.

"It's a three-part assignment, and y'all may divvy the responsibilities however you like. First, someone must write a two-page monologue on 'what it means to be you.' I want y'all to put a lot of thought into this! Really dig deep."

Grumbles and groans chorus around the room, but a lopsided grin takes over my face. Hopefully Wynn and Sully don't mind letting me tackle the monologue—a surefire win for me.

"Then, you will design a small set and costumes, and perform the monologue in front of an audience of your choice. It can be just me or in front of the whole class. This will account for twenty-five percent of your grade this semester. Discuss roles among your groups until bell, then I'll see you hooligans tomorrow!"

Wynn wastes no time seizing my bicep, eyes glimmering. "You don't mind if I perform, do you? I mean—it's fine if you do, we'll just have to battle to the death over it."

I snort. "I left my sword at home. You can have it."

Wynn does a bouncy victory dance that makes the rubber fish lures in her stockings jiggle, and I can't help but smile. I turn to Sully, who's gazing at me with a wince that says he definitely has a preference for his role in the project. Our faces must be twinning, because as he studies me, he cracks up.

"You first."

"I really hate clothes," I confess. "Please don't make me design costumes."

"I really hate writing," he says solemnly. "And you can take costumes out of my cold, rigor mortis hands."

"Perfect. Go team!" I say, giggling.

"Cool boots," Sully remarks.

Wynn nods in agreement, then shoves her warm, rosy arm through the crook of mine. "Sooooo, welcome to Brightbarrel Middle! We're your friends now."

Behind her, my shadow yawns, stands, and takes a dramatic bow.

Fine, I think. I did the thing, and everything turned out okay. Not only do I actually *like* Sully and Wynn? I also have a feeling we're going to ace this project. I tip an imaginary hat to Shadow. *You win this one, creep face.*

Chapter Six
Sparrow Connecting Dots

Sparrow Malone

Mr. Fullilove

Science Essay, Seventh Grade

Mutualism is a kind of cooperative relationship between two different species, in which both benefit from working together toward a common goal. "I scratch your back, you scratch mine" or "It's a win-win!" are both sayings that have the spirit of mutualism.

My favorite example is between humans and wild African birds called honeyguides. (The "wild" part is important because these birds aren't trained pets!) Honeyguides love to eat honeycomb wax, and they work with human honey-hunters by calling and leading them to the bees' nests inside baobab trees. The humans use smoke and tools to subdue the hives and retrieve the honey (since birds aren't so handy with axes), and both the honey-hunters and the honeyguides get something from the deal. African researchers, with the help of honey-hunters, continue to study the relationship between humans and honeyguides, to discover more about mutualism.

Thursday night is a chaotic scramble to prepare for my first full day of school. I try on a few T-shirts Mags bought while I was in drama and reorganize my writing folder for the thirteenth time. Then, I gobble down dinner, shower, and let Mags put my hair in a braid before I fall into bed exhausted. I don't see the exact moment Shadow disappears, but when I finally notice it's gone, I heave a sigh of relief. "Nature is healing," I say, patting my brain before conking out like a light.

When I wake in the morning, Shadow is still nowhere to be seen.

I'm halfway through a bowl of shredded wheat—cranky and bedraggled because I fell asleep without setting an alarm—when there's a banging at Mags's door. Bela Pugosi flies into a hysterical barking fit, peeing on the doormat a little.

"Mind getting that, Sparrow?" Mags calls, her hand over her phone. "I think it's for you!"

My first thought is *Mom's here!* even though that's impossible. "Calm down, Bela Pugosi, or your little pug eyes might pop out. The internet says that's called proptosis. Can you say 'proptosis'? Gotta tell you, buddy—it doesn't look like fun," I grump, trudging to the door.

I try to see through the peephole, but it's clouded over with grime. Which means I'm forced to yank the door open so Bela will stop his yipping.

Standing on the doormat is Wynn from drama. This catches me off-guard, so I gape instead of saying hi. Wynn is clad in a loose white T-shirt with flowers—actual fresh flowers—stitched onto the front with embroidery thread. She literally has mums, dahlias, and orange lilies sewn right on, like a complete maniac. It's bizarre, and I love it. Wynn notices me noticing and is obviously pleased. She shoots a peace sign and grins.

"Hey! Wanna walk to the bus stop together?"

I do, but I have questions. "Wait, how'd you get here? Did someone drop you off?" Does Mags think I need baby-sitting on the bus or something? Do I seem that helpless?

"Walked." Wynn points to the double-wide with a wheelchair ramp beside Mags's trailer—the one with black flowers and dismembered doll parts. "That's me and Dad, right there! Dad's a professor at the community college with Mags. He teaches art."

That makes sense, and the disoriented cobwebs slowly disentangle from my mood. "So we're neighbors," I explain to myself.

"Go get your bag!" Wynn commands, laughing. "We're gonna miss the bus!"

I nod and dash away, running to my room and double-checking my book bag for my writing folder. I avoid myself in the mirror—my jeans are too short, but what can you do? I jam my feet into my new boots, tighten the laces, and dash for the door. I nearly trip when Shadow unspools itself from my feet and stretches, like it just woke up. *So much for not seeing things anymore.*

Wynn's shrill voice blasts through the house. "Eight minutes!"

I gallop through the trailer, rattling windowpanes and dishes, and rejoin Wynn outside. Shadow is sharp in the sunlight as it does a wild pirouette on the dew-kissed grass. I force my attention on Wynn. "So, did you do the shirt yourself?"

"I did! I've gotten good with a needle. Sully's teaching me."

"And . . . won't the flowers be dead by the end of the day?"

"Yes," says Wynn with a knowing look. "You get it."

I do not, in fact, get it. I raise my eyebrows and smile a little. "It's . . . that's just so much work for something that only lasts a few hours!"

"Right? But people only notice the work that goes into clothes when they're the ones making them. They just toss them out every season for the newest trend," Wynn rants as she walks, sweeping her hands. "Plus, lots of cloth today doesn't even biodegrade, so then what? It just piles up in dumps."

"Or at Trader Jolene's," I offer, starting to understand. Wynn must have made this shirt for a research assignment— maybe science or social studies?

"Yeah, I guess," Wynn says, frowning. "But at least there, people use them again." She glances quietly over my outfit, and I squirm. I hate feeling noticed, especially by people my age. It's like someone is reading one of my half-written essays.

"So, do you think you'll get an A?" I ask, hugging myself.

"On what?"

I jerk my chin at her shirt. "Your project."

Wynn wrinkles her nose. "Oh, this? It isn't for school. It's performance art, just for me! It's one of my hobbies." Wynn starts listing things on her fingers. "I also do photography, make sculptures for the garden, Rollerblade, and I'm really into Junji Ito's horror manga. What are you into?"

"I'm kind of obsessed with animals and nature," I admit. "And I watch old monster movies sometimes. *Creature from the Black Lagoon* is my favorite."

"Oh, awesome! What else?"

A breeze sets off a chorus of homemade wind chimes across the garden. The clanks from metal forks, tinkling shells, and sweet little rusty bells sync for a minute as if in concert. Shadow darts in front of me and mimes singing into a hairbrush, passionately clutching its heart and running a

hand through its wild hair. The moves are painfully familiar. I blush.

"Oh," I mumble. "I guess . . . I guess I sing and dance
sometimes."

"In choir?"

"Absolutely never in choir," I say, grinning. "In the
shower. Only when Mom's gone." And then I realize I not
only just brought up my mom but also the fact that I'm
home alone sometimes—something I'm not supposed to do.
I wince. *Please don't ask questions*, I think.

"That's chill." Wynn smiles, offering a fist bump.
"Me too."

We've reached the bus stop by the main road, just in time
for the rumbling behemoth to arrive. I've never ridden the bus
before—Mom's always had a thing about wanting to drive me.
I hide my excitement as I hop on behind Wynn, my shadow
just barely slipping through the doors before they shriek shut.

The bus? It's basically the same noises, manners, and
smells of a school hallway, compressed into a sardine can on
wheels. Nothing to get excited about.

But the rest of the day is a wild ride that consumes every
last drop of my attention and energy. There's no time to
watch Shadow clown as I scribble notes, blow away a math

skill assessment test, study my teachers, and collect assignments into the welcoming jaws of my three-ring binder. It's discouraging, watching my peers turn in homework while I'm empty-handed, but that's okay. Come Monday I'll be armed to the teeth with completed papers and extra credit.

I don't see Kylie in math since I was in the hallway for assessment. During lunch period, though, someone hip checks me in the line for sloppy joes. My fingers clench as I whirl, expecting more of Shadow's obnoxiousness. I relax when I see Kylie there, smirking. "Hey." My heart is a flopping trout in my chest.

"Hey yourself."

"I'm mad at you, you know," she says, slurping a juice box.

"You don't look mad."

Kylie nudges my boot with her foot. "C'mon, play along!"

"Okayyy. Why are you mad?"

"Because you sat in the hallway all period, and no one was around to save me from a marauding band of exponents."

My neck flames. This is a compliment of some sort—I can tell by the way Kylie's smiling right into my eyes. Barely blinking, too, like she enjoys watching me get flustered. I glance at Shadow, who's making heart hands. What do I say next? "I, uh—I can sit at your table and rescue you now, if you want." I want to add "m'lady," but worry that might be too much. Because we're friends, Mom. Just friends.

Kylie sighs. "Wish I could! I told my youth group girls I'd sit with them—Mia's parents are going through a thing."

I don't know who Mia is, but I get it. "Maybe some other time, then." A few tables over, Sully waves at me from where he's saved me a spot. I grin and wave back, relieved. At least I have somewhere to sit.

"You could come to my house tomorrow."

I swallow, considering how I would even navigate that with Mags. We haven't really talked about rules with friends yet. Then I realize I can't say yes anyway, because Mom's calling sometime on Saturday. "I can't tomorrow—wish I could. But I have plans."

Kylie grins and shrugs. "It's fine. Anyway, my mom got Trevor M—he's a boy in math class—moved from the seat beside me today, because he breathes too loud and won't stop annoying me. Annnd"—she draws the word out dramatically—"after class I told Teacher Jones I'd volunteer to let the new kid sit beside me."

"That was nice! Lucky new kid," I say honestly.

"You're such a goob. That's you, silly. See you in class on Monday!"

Her wavy ponytail swings as she walks away. Kylie has an incredibly determined walk, I notice. Like she's someone's boss, or an Olympic champion, or a fully-armed Valkyrie from *Thor: Ragnarok. Better add that to the list of things about her that render me as soft as a jellyfish.* I putter carefully through foot traffic until I get to Sully, where Shadow is already dancing on the table.

"Someone has a crush," Sully sings softly as I sit down.

I'm sure my face goes as red as my hair. "What? Who? *No, ew.* That's crazy talk."

"Kylie's nice," Sully says slyly, shrugging a thin shoulder. "Nothing to be ashamed of." He carefully peels the crusts off a cucumber sandwich—no sloppy joes for him, I guess. Sully's neat fingernails are all painted perfectly in a grayish purple except for the pinkies, which are painted perfectly in banana-slug-yellow. Shadow sits and scoots closer to Sully, mesmerized by his dangly silver sword earring.

Okay, I think. *Maybe I'm crushing hard on Kylie, but Mom would worry if she thought people knew.* So, I need to know how to hide it better. I bury my face in my hands and peek sheepishly out at Sully between my fingers. "What gave it away?"

Sully tilts his chair back and laughs triumphantly. "See? I knew it! I'm never wrong about these things."

"Seriously, though. How'd you know?"

"Your eyebrows jump when you see her," Sully begins, leaning forward and lowering his voice. "And the whole time y'all were talking, you hung on her every word." He demonstrates, pulling a serious, intense face that's supposed to look like me.

"That could just be good listening," I counter, crossing my arms.

"Yeah, maybe. Except when you're talking to anyone else, I've noticed your brain whirring, staying a step ahead of them. You're always thinking instead of listening," Sully says, then dramatically bites his sandwich for emphasis.

"Okay, that's just rude, Sully." *And not wrong*, I realize. Ouch.

"But you can't do that around people you're crushing on, because you get flustered."

I eye him warily. *He's probably a witch*, I decide. "How are you so good at this?"

"I'm the baby of the family." Sully grins, puffing out his chest. "Three sisters in college. You learn fast. And I'm quiet, which makes me a good observer."

I can't take this much scrutiny, so I turn the tables. "So, what do you do when you like someone?"

Sully goes shy. "I don't. Like someone. I don't like people in that way."

I lower my voice. "Not . . . girls *or* boys?"

"Nope."

"I guess I just thought—" I clam up because I don't know what I thought, exactly. Because he had painted nails, maybe I guessed Sully likes guys or something? Or maybe it's because he didn't blink when he knew I liked Kylie. "I'm sorry, I guess I just assumed things."

"Don't break your brain, Sparrow," Sully says, giggling. "It's okay to not know everything." He pulls out his cell phone. "Wanna see my family?"

We spend the rest of lunch scrolling through photos of Sully's family. They have a tiny polka-dot poodle named Confetti, and two bright-colored macaws. Sully's parents are both older than Mom, with stylish glasses and relaxed smiles. "They met in grad school," Sully explains. "Then they both earned doctorates in sustainable agriculture. Mom grew up in Kansas City, and Dad's from South Carolina. They argue about barbecue a lot."

I nod, laughing. My mom has strong opinions when it

comes to regional barbecue, too: *"When I pass into the next life, just bury me in a vat of vinegar-based barbecue sauce."* I don't mention it to Sully, but it feels good to remember that Mom and I actually have fun together sometimes. Lately, it feels like everyone—even me—has focused on the bad stuff. I swallow down a guilty lump as Sully keeps scrolling.

In his selfies taken at home, I notice Sully wears flowy cardigans sometimes, or skirts with tights underneath. He always looks so stylish, and I find myself studying him like a puzzle. How did he get so comfortable in his skin? How do his clothes always seem to love him so much?

I'm curious if Sully feels at home as a guy, or if he's more like my Aunt Mags, but it feels like the sort of thing I shouldn't just ask. Like it's too personal? I wish there were someone, though, I could ask some of these questions to without dying of embarrassment. Because it feels like I should already know this stuff.

The rest of the day is a blur, ending in drama. Everyone crowds onto the big rug, sitting crisscross with their notebooks. Wynn practically yanks me onto the floor, squeezed between her and Sully. My heart flutters over feeling like I have *a spot*, but I try to play it cool, like this happens to me all the time.

Mr. Fitz clears his throat. Today, he's wearing a ridiculous stuffed jester's hat with bells on the end, but his face is as serious as sin. A few people struggle not to giggle, and he glares at them in mock sternness. "All right, y'all, without overthinking it, you have ten minutes to write one paragraph in first person about a favorite memory. One, two, three, *go!*"

Pencils and pens scribble furiously around me as I flip to a page and write the date. Then, my brain freezes. For two whole minutes—120 agonizing blank seconds—I can't think of anything at all. My pits are damp, and I worry they're making dark rings on my shirt. A gray hand creeps around my shoulder and cups my grip on the pencil. *Geez, Shadow.* I hold my breath, completely freaked out, while I watch my hand write *The Ferris Wheel Incident* at the top of the page. Shadow lets go, then sits politely on the rug.

Oh, no way—I do not have a death wish. If I wrote about that, Mom might actually strangle me. When I was little, she got distracted on her cell phone at the county fair and the bored teenager taking tickets let me ride the wheel alone.

Recounting the Ferris Wheel Incident is high on Mom's list of Thou Shalt Nots because she thinks it makes her sound like a crummy parent. So however Shadow knows about that memory, it should also know that writing about it is a terrible suggestion. But now, as I try to come up with another memory, all I can see in my head are spinning Ferris wheels.

"Five minutes left," announces Mr. Fitz.

Fine. Just this once, because I need this grade, I'll follow Shadow's suggestion. I scribble furiously about the day I accidentally rode the county fair's Ferris wheel by myself when I was little, because Mom was distracted by a text in line. Chewing the inside of my mouth in concentration, I whip out an amazing paragraph in four minutes. I hug my knees while I wait for Mr. Fitz to call time.

"All right, gang," he chirps. "Now, I'd like to challenge someone to read their paragraph aloud, adding facial expressions and body language to match the emotions in the paragraph. I won't force anyone, but I will remind you that willingness to participate counts for part of your grade. Who's first?"

A seasick feeling grips me. *Raise your hand*, I tell myself. I need Mr. Fitz to think I'm fearless. Beside me, Wynn flails her arm like she's trying to slap the ceiling.

"Miss Soderlund, you're up!" Wynn hops to her feet and jogs front and center. She starts her paragraph, subtle emotion playing across her face effortlessly. But I can't hear what she's saying, because blood is busy whooshing through my ears. Everything around me seems strange and garbled.

I should go next, I tell myself over and over, fingers picking away at my cuticles. My stomach feels like I'm eating spicy pickled okra on a roller coaster. Shadow scuttles down from the ceiling and creeps toward me, cocking its head to the side.

Everyone claps, and Wynn plops next to me again, face rosy and pleased. Sully reaches in front of me, fist-bumping her in congrats. *Here we go*, I think. My muscles tense like a track runner at the starting blocks. Mr. Fitz barely has time to say, "So, who's nex—" when I jump to my feet, legs wobbling.

"Ooookay, then." Mr. Fitz chuckles. "We've got an eager group this afternoon!"

My knees almost give out as I walk forward, but I grind my teeth and clench my notebook in determination. I force a pleasant look onto my face and swallow hard.

"When I was sheven, my mom take—*took*—me to the

fair," I force out. My words are doing their jumbled thing again, and frustration flares in my chest.

"Take your time, Sparrow!" Mr. Fitz calls softly. "It's perfectly normal to take a moment to focus."

I breathe in-two-three-four, out-two-three-four, then do it again. The room gets sharper, and my arms and legs start to feel real again.

"I was captivated by the winking lights and the slow rotation of the Ferris wheel, because it reminded me of Christmas, even though it was summer," I continue. *Um, Sparrow? You're supposed to be acting out your feelings*, I remind myself. But when I try to express them, it's so much harder than putting them in my notebook. My mouth is bone-dry, and I panic giggle.

Shadow, who's sitting directly in front of me on the rug like an obedient student (instead of some terrifying nightmare ghoul), stands and inches forward until we're nose-to-nose. It's impossible to ignore those blazing orb eyes when they're a hair away from my face. No one else sees it. Everyone is staring at *me*, concern building in a few of their faces.

I cough and read the next sentence. "The wheel seemed

like a gigantic Christmas ornament you could ride, and I decided sitting at the top would be like flying."

As I read, Shadow tilts back its head and reaches skyward, feet wide apart. I stand there perspiring, my arms stiff at my sides. A kid to my right groans in secondhand embarrassment. Shadow flails at me, then mimes pointing at the sky again.

On a desperate impulse, I copy Shadow. As my finger points, I feel a flitter of Ferris-wheel excitement. As we come to the bit about flying, Shadow slowly closes its orb eyes like a happy cat and spreads its arms wide. As I let myself mirror it, my mind's eye sparkles with rotating lights that shine against an orange-and-purple sunset. I'm seven, at the fair again with sticky cotton-candy fingers. I steal a glance at Wynn, and she nods for me to keep going.

Together, Shadow and I reenact how terrified I was, stuck on the wheel alone. We show getting closer to Mom each time my seat descended and watching her shrink away as the wheel swung up again. We act out Mom, panicked for the first several rotations, then relaxing and taking my picture with her phone as I passed. We show how I was on top of the world by the end of the ride and wished it had lasted longer.

When I finish, the classroom breaks into clapping. Mr. Fitz nods approvingly in his jingling jester hat. "See how much it helps to give yourself a moment or two? Nice work, Sparrow."

I hurry to my seat. Sully and Wynn whisper and poke me in congratulations, and I grin. Shadow still hovers at the front of the room. I decide to be polite to my hallucination, and I mouth, *"thank you."*

Maybe . . . it's not purely evil, I decide. More like chaotic neutral.

Chapter Seven

Sparrow Scheming

Sparrow Malone

Mr. Fullilove

Science Essay, Seventh Grade

What Is a Keystone Species?

In architecture, when builders construct an arc, the top stone—the keystone—is considered the most important. All the other blocks are held in tension by this final wedge-shaped rock, and they rely on the keystone for stability. Take away this important piece, and everything risks falling into a pile of rubble.

In a similar way, many organisms within an eco-system may rely on a single species—a keystone species—to provide stability for the whole group. Bees are a good example of a keystone species, since they pollinate plants and trees. The plants rely on bees for pollination, and insects, mammals, birds, and reptiles depend upon the plants for food and shelter. If a keystone species disappears, then the whole ecosystem might start to unravel.

The second I get home from school, I kick off my boots just inside the door and wiggle my toes. The moment I do, Shadow disappears.

"No way," I whisper. I hustle to my bedroom for privacy, where I conduct an experiment.

I tug on a boot and wait, breathing hard. The inky, me-shaped puddle rises from the floor just feet away from me, staring with its uncanny headlight eyes. I lift a hand, and Shadow mirrors me. I wave fast, then stop suddenly and make a rude gesture. Shadow stops mimicking me and puts a palm to its forehead in exasperation.

I pull my foot from the boot. Shadow vanishes.

Interesting. When I'm wearing my new boots, Shadow comes to life. But what *is* it?

Several times now, Shadow has nudged me toward doing something I know would annoy Mom: geeking out over horror novels, sharing my love for singing at home alone with Wynn, and now writing about the Ferris Wheel Incident in class.

I grab my notebook and scribble: *Shadow—a bad influence??*

But then I stop myself. Didn't those things pay off? I hit it off with my drama team, which will probably result in an awesome grade. And thanks to mirroring Shadow, I didn't bomb my reading this afternoon. Mr. Fitz thinks I'm actually good at acting. I write: *But Shadow also might help me save Mom.*

I frown, thinking. Does Shadow trade a Thou Shalt Not for a favor? Is that how this works? Maybe it's like . . . a bargain of some kind. If Shadow's hungry for broken rules and willing to help me, why not use that to my advantage? Well, mine *and* Mom's.

Maybe it's worth it, if it means I get Mom back faster. And if things get out of control, I can always take the boots off.

"This is all in my head," I inform my boots. "And I still

love you, even if you're making me hallucinate." Despite everything, I can't wait to put them back on tomorrow and feel my heart sing in my chest when I spot myself in the mirror. This knowledge burns a guilty path from my throat all the way to my guts. Because how would Mom feel if she knew I was experimenting with forbidden shoes and delicious butterfly feelings while she's stuck in some strange room without me?

Almost automatically, I'm up and walking toward the living room. Mags sits in a folding chair with bifocals poised on her nose as she studies some papers. Before she notices me, my eagle eye spots my mom's name at the top of a page. It's an official-looking report of some kind. I clear my throat. "Hey, Aunt Mags?"

Mags looks up and quickly turns the papers facedown. "Heya! What's cookin', good lookin'?"

"Any news from my mom yet?" I hate that my voice sounds this pitiful and small. But the anxious thrum in my chest is awful, like a broken record stuck on *Mom! Mom! Mom!* I know it would ease up if I could just talk to her. Aunt Mags's eyes go soft.

"She's calling on Saturday, love! I know she misses you so much. You're a pretty amazing kiddo."

Dang it, Aunt Mags. I don't want to cry, but the gentleness in her voice makes tears sting my nose. *Here's a safe place to land*, Mags's kindness offers. But I'm not ready to admit I'm falling yet. If I hold out a little longer, things will be okay. Mom will recover, I'll go back to normal, and I won't have to talk about *feelings*.

Mags seems to get it and changes the subject. "So, how do you feel about meeting the rest of your new Rainbow House neighbors? No rain tonight, so a lot of folks are doing bean soup and a bonfire."

"Maybe tomorrow," I hedge. Because what's the point of meeting more people I'll never see again in a few months? And who makes bonfires this often anyway? Besides, I still need to get a jump start on writing my monologue for drama. As I walk out of the room, I hear Mags's rolltop desk open and shut as she puts the papers away.

Back in the bedroom, I whip out a notebook and pencil, sprawl onto the carpet, and set to work on my drama monologue. But by the time I have the first paragraph, the paper is covered in eraser marks and it's getting close to sundown. Stretching my elbows toward the ceiling, I yawn and frown down at my piddly four sentences. It never takes me this long to write. Why do I have snails for brains?

Through the window, firelight flickers across the sprawling garden. Shrieks of playful laughter peal through the night like bottle rockets. The voices sound young. *One of them is probably Wynn*, I realize. Everyone's having fun, but don't they have homework? A soft knock at the door makes me jump.

"Room service," Luca announces. He balances a wooden tray of steaming pinto beans, corn bread, and a glass of iced tea. "No good thoughts happen on an empty stomach, amore," he fusses. "Come to the kitchen if you need more!" I thank him politely and shut the door again with a socked foot.

I like Luca. He and Mags make sense together, like butter and corn bread. His enormous eyebrows and mustache dance like three happy caterpillars every time she walks into the room, and I find myself wondering if anyone will ever look at me like that.

Someday, if I ever have a mustache, I'll keep mine trimmed smaller, I decide, then freeze, spoon halfway to my mouth. *Blink, blink.* Why did I just think that? Of course I won't have a mustache. Just like I never went as Spider-Man on Halloween or visited a motel swimming pool bare chested. Just like I won't actually buzz my hair. These thoughts whoosh through their well-worn path in my brain so quickly, it's almost an involuntary motion, like swallowing.

Ugh. My sides ache from sudden fullness, and I slide the dinner tray beneath my bed. I give up monologue writing, just for tonight. I could work on my keystone species observation report for science, instead. I could probably tackle it in an hour or two. But what species could I sneak out and observe tonight? There's just a little daylight left.

I crack my door and listen. Silence. Mags and Luca must've gone to the bonfire. I shuffle into the living room, pausing for a second in front of the rolltop desk. The papers from Mom's accident—and probably her trip to rehab— are in there. Part of me wants to snoop, but Mom's always hated it.

Probably to keep me out of her purse, I think. So I'd stay away from the medications there, especially the ones that weren't really hers. "Too bad she couldn't stay away from them herself," I mutter, ignoring my instant guilt.

There's no one to stop me from poking around now, is there? Just Mom's voice in my head, and her unofficial list of Thou Shalt Nots: no haircuts, no "ugly" clothes, no weirdos, no horror movies, no spiders, no shut doors, no bats, no spitting, no beets, no sleepovers, no country music, no questions about the past . . .

I think Mom knows it's silly to officially forbid something like eating a vegetable, but that doesn't stop her from acting like I've disappointed her to the core when I cross her preferences. It unsettles her, and unsettling Mom? It's the Malones' deadliest sin. It almost feels like bad luck.

Despite all this, my left hand inches toward the desk knob, but a sick, twisting feeling—dread?—reels it back toward my body again.

Not tonight, I decide.

Instead, I lace up my boots and scurry outside with my notebook. Shadow follows, a near-translucent smudge in the peachy light. Cicadas whirr from the trees like angry little clockwork gods counting down the days to colder weather. A bittersweet breeze drifts across the flower beds that border the rambling patchwork garden, relieving my sweaty neck from the humidity. I inhale and trudge to the end of the clearing farthest from the bonfire gathering. I've got no time for fake smiling.

Shadow weaves in and out of wire-wreathed tomato plants and wooden planter boxes teeming with herbs. It stops to bury its face in a rosemary bush or to catch gently swaying honeysuckle vines between eager shadow-fingers. I'm careful where I step, not wanting to upset anything.

I scan the edge of the woods, hoping to spot an animal darting. There are plants on the keystone species list, of course, but I'm more of a fauna person. Dropping my knees to a dry patch of grass, I crouch on all fours next to a row of purple flowers and squint, hoping to spot some straggling bees.

I nearly topple when an elongated arm explodes from the bush inches from my face, fingers splayed. "Dangit, Shadow!" I hiss. Its finger crooks in a "follow me!" gesture. I shudder as it slithers back through the stems, and Shadow emerges on the other side, running away from me. I stall for a split second, heart thumping. Then I remember my plan to humor Shadow in exchange for Shadow's good luck, and curiosity gets the better of me. I crouch-run, praying no one spots me.

Shadow slides to a halt beneath a row of enormous, flattened birdhouses that rest atop wooden poles. It spins in delight and then shimmies up the nearest one. When it waves me up, I shake my head. I could climb up after it—easily, thank you very much—but between the two of us, Shadow's less likely to get punished for it. *Being pretend and all.*

"They're bat boxes," a cheerful voice calls, and I nearly choke on my chewing gum.

I look over my shoulder to see two young people sitting in a clover patch behind me, holding hands. They disentangle themselves and wave, grinning. One has brown, freckled skin, glasses, and shaggy hair, and the other's wearing a baseball cap and a bandana. They're both in tank tops with a college logo on the front.

"Sorry, I—I didn't realize anyone was here," I stammer. "Wait, did you say *bats*?"

"Little brown bats!" says the one with the glasses, nodding. Tiny silver balls decorate the deep dimples of their friendly round cheeks. "They're coming out any minute. It's really cool, you should watch with us! But you might want to back up a little."

The Windy Hall bats. When my mom was a kid, her parents would ground her to the attic for acting out. Bats often tried to roost there, coming in through a hole in the vent—Mom's been terrified of them since. Still, according

101

to my handout from science class, they're a keystone species for this area. Good-grade fodder for sure. I pretend I'm not nervous.

"How many are there?" I ask, fiddling my pencil out from the notebook spiral and sitting down several feet away from the couple. Shadow slides down from the bat house and creeps closer. "Like, more than five bats?"

"Ohhhh, you're in for a treat! Way more than five," the shorter one says, removing the ball cap and raking stubby fingers through sweaty blond hair. "They used to roost in the rafters of Rainbow House until Professor Malone had me seal them off and we built the bat houses. The little brown bats took right to them—we totally lucked out! This colony has managed to avoid white-nose syndrome—that's a fungus deadly to bats. So it's a good-sized group."

It takes me a second to realize "Professor Malone" means Aunt Mags. I smile shyly. "I'm Sparrow Malone. Mags is my aunt."

Baseball Cap grins. "Sparrow's a cool name!"

"I picked it myself," I blurt, then instantly regret it. Why did I say that?

"Hey, that's cool. I picked my name, too! I'm November,"

Baseball Cap says, then points to the one with the glasses. "And this is my classmate-roommate-sweetheart hybrid, Azul. We study plant science at Mountainview College. We both live in the old Rainbow House this year."

I think Azul's a girl, probably. But this whole time, my brain's been toggling back and forth, trying to tell if November's a guy or not. Their arms are strong and sinewy with little tattoos here and there, even on their fingers. *But both guys* and *girls can be buff,* I remind myself. My last gym teacher, Mrs. Montanez, made sure we were all familiar with powerful athletes like gymnast Simone Biles, soccer player Marta Vieira da Silva, and WNBA player Brittney Griner.

My eyes comb for more clues, and I think Shadow's trying to guess, too. November's ears are pierced in a dozen different places, sparkling in the fading orange light. They have fuzzy legs. Their fingernails are painted neon green, the color of baby ferns. *Girl? But Sully's a boy who paints his nails,* I remind myself. So that just means November likes polish. Why is this bugging me? Does it matter? We all sit in silence for a minute, watching the bat boxes.

"So, how'd you choose November for your name?" I finally blurt. I'm honestly curious. And the trickster in me is hoping they'll say something that'll tell me if they're a "he" or "she," without me having to ask.

November grins and holds up both hands, wiggling their fingers. On the left hand, their index finger is completely missing. "November means nine," they say, laughing.

I think for a beat, then ask, "Then why's it the eleventh month on the calendar?"

They both grin, and November whoops in approval. "I like this kid!"

Azul shoves November playfully. "You can't say that and not explain, silly. Sparrow, it's because the Roman calendar originally had ten months, so November was the ninth way back when. You asked a good question."

I grin wide. I like the way Azul and November flirt with each other, eyes warm and shoulders loose, both secure enough to let their guards down. My mind wanders to Kylie, trying to picture us together, laughing and relaxed. I blush and herd my attention back to the present. "Makes sense." These people? They're super nerds. And I just said something that impressed them. Not only do I feel like I just swallowed the sun, I also really like them back.

The flaming late summer sunset fades to a whisper, all dusty lilac ribboned in fuzzy-peach clouds. I swat a mosquito and try not to stare at November and Azul anymore, because I do actually have manners. We wait quietly, and I scribble down notes detailing the time and place of my bat observation.

My pencil's just done scratching when I hear tiny, high-pitched shrieks overhead. Shadow leaps up from the grass and points, losing its mind with excitement as little flapping bodies emerge from the bat boxes.

I don't know what I expected—they're called *little* brown bats, after all. But from Mom's description, I'd imagined vampire fangs and spiteful talons eager to scratch out my eyes. These are more like flying hamsters, streaming out of the boxes and zigzagging across the garden. A shiver crawls down my spine anyway—it's like Mom's bad memories have written themselves into my DNA. I force my lungs to work slower. *In-two-three-four, out-two-three-four.* "The bats are tiny," I finally whisper.

"They really are," November says softly, grinning open-mouthed as Azul squints at the sky intently, then scribbles numbers in a notebook. "A grown adult only weighs about the same as three pennies."

"But they're amazing for the garden," Azul adds, not looking up from her writing. "A mama with babies can eat almost her body weight in a night! They like to munch potato beetles, squash beetles, mosquitoes, and invasive emerald ash borer beetles . . . They're basically guardians of the garden and forest."

Shadow is kneeling right under the boxes, head turned upward, completely transfixed.

"That's why they're a keystone species," I mutter. "They do pest control."

"They're endangered, too, poor things. Humans keep accidentally introducing fungus into their caves. Bats are a social species, like people, and they stick together when they roost. They snuggle up and infect each other without meaning to."

"That's so sad," I murmur.

I scribble observations in shorthand—I can pretty them up later. The last of the bats emerge and fly off into the night. Azul stretches and pecks November on the cheek. "That's it for me! Big exam in the morning. Ready to walk back, love?"

November nods. "You going back to the bonfire, Sparrow? We don't want to leave you out here alone in the dark."

I shake my head. "No bonfire, just the trailer. I have homework."

"We'll walk you back to Professor M's on our way to Rainbow House, then."

I nod in agreement, and the three of us begin to walk. I'm secretly happy to spend more time around November. It's not that I have a puppy crush on them or anything—they're ancient as dirt compared to me. My fascination is more like seeing a color I never knew existed. They're graceful and strong, pretty and handsome, this *and* that—and I kind of want to cry but in a good way? Like I'm relieved, but I can't understand why.

I'm worried I won't pluck up the courage to say hi again after tonight, and then I'll never figure it out. Shadow sneaks up behind me and nudges my back, as if to say: *Go on!* I shiver. I'll never get used to Shadow's uncanny mind-reading ability. When I shake my head, Shadow pokes me again, harder. *Say something.*

"November?" I blurt. "Um, my science teacher said I could do a garden project for extra credit if one of the botany students here supervised me." My heart knocks against my sternum, and my fingers buzz. Mom has a strict "no weirdos" rule, which I'm now thinking is a pretty harsh way to describe someone. November and Azul are smart and kind—should it make a difference how they dress or wear their hair?

"Sooo, you want to know if Azul and me can help you?"

I nod, hugging my notebook harder.

November scowls deeply and strokes their chin. "Tricky question. I'll need to go home and consult my cat, and my calendar, and our Magic Eight Ball . . ."

I gulp, waiting.

"Ignore them," Azul says, playfully popping the brim of November's hat. "They're trying to be funny, and they're gonna hurt themselves. We'd be happy to help you, Sparrow."

November's scowl cracks into a grin. "Just be sure it's okay with your aunt Mags, first, and then we'll work out some times."

But I'm stuck on what Azul said. *Them. They.* I've been using "them" in my head to think about November, because I didn't know which pronoun was right for them. But obviously, if they're sweethearts, Azul would know which words to use. Which means . . . November really is *they.* Does this mean they're also not a guy *or* a girl? I realize Azul and November have been waiting forever for me to respond.

"Awesome." I grin. "Thanks! I'm pretty sure Mags will say yes, since it was her idea."

"Ask anyway," Azul says as the two of them peel off in the direction of Windy Hall. *Rainbow House*, I think, because I like it better. "Communication is always good."

I wave goodbye before I slip back into Mags and Luca's trailer. Shadow circles me in a victory strut, and I work hard to suppress a giggle. I don't want to look bat-guano nuts in front of my new tutors. I wait for them to be out of earshot before I turn and speak.

"All right, Shadow," I whisper before taking my boots off at the door. "Here's the deal. I'll make a list of things Mom hates, since it seems like you love seeing me break them. And I will, but *only* the things on the list. And only as long as you help me do good in school and at home with Mags, so I can help Mom snap out of it. A trade for a grade. Got it?"

Shadow shrinks a bit. Its glowing eyes blink in consideration. Then, slowly, it nods and shrugs.

I lick my lips. "It's a deal, then."

I go inside and scribble the list for Shadow.

no bats

no beets

no country music

no "ugly" clothes

no sleepovers

no weirdos

no questions about the past

no snooping

no haircuts

I stare at it for a long while before chickening out, then crumpling it up and throwing it into the trash bin.

Chapter Eight
Sparrow Making Deals

Sparrow's notebook

The first mammal in space wasn't a human at all. It was a monkey named Albert II, sent into space on a rocket by the United States in 1949. He didn't ask to go, and he probably didn't understand what was happening at all. Albert didn't really get a choice and unfortunately didn't survive reentry. Poor Albert didn't even understand what was happening!

Humans make strange choices sometimes.

Saturday morning, I'm ruined for anything but waiting for Mom's call. I sit on my hands in the armchair, then go stand by the window, then it's back to the armchair, bouncing my knees anxiously.

Thirty more minutes. Twenty-five. Fifteen.

My stomach can't decide if it's starving or the exact opposite, so I only pick at Luca's polenta—basically grits, Italian style—and bacon. By the time Wynn drops by to see if I want to come over for video games, it's only five minutes until Mom's call, and I have Mags send Wynn away. Finally, Mags's phone buzzes, and my heart leaps into my throat.

"Hi, this is Mags!" Mags pauses, then says, "All right, I understand. It's so good to hear from you. Here's Sparrow."

I grab the phone and head to my bedroom. Mags doesn't follow, giving me some privacy. "Hello?"

"Maggie Grace, baby, it's so good to hear your voice!" Mom's voice sounds froggy, like she's been crying, and she's using the funny baby tone she sometimes does when she means to sound parental. It mostly just makes her sound vulnerable, though, and a painful ball gathers in my voice box.

I want to curl up and sob on my bed. Talking to Mom again floods me with wild feelings that are almost too overwhelming for my body. *Be strong*, I tell myself.

"Hey, Mama," I chirp, because I know she likes it when I call her that. A tear pops out of my eye and rolls down my cheek, but that's fine because she can't see it. "Things are going great here—I made a couple of friends at school! All my teachers bragged on my good manners."

Mom's voice is watery, almost a whine. "Well, I just hate it that you have to stay at that place, baby. These people don't understand"—her voice cracks, and I can hear a rush of jagged air in the receiver—"it was just all such a mix-up. I took the wrong medication for a headache, and I'm just so sorry I can't be with you right now."

My fingers tighten around the cell phone. *A mix-up.* I know this probably isn't true, and she's just trying to protect me, but part of me wants to believe her. Because what if it really was a mistake? My rib cage puffs out, and I feel the urge to punch someone—to protect my mom from anything and anyone that would make her cry.

"It's going to be okay, Mom. Just start feeling better, and do whatever you need to. Everything will be all right soon!"

"I'm just so afraid they're going to take you away," Mom's voice whimpers, then just as quickly strengthens into something with more steel in it. "Are those people being good to you? Are they treating you right, Maggie?"

Sparrow, a tiny part of my brain corrects. "Yeah, Mom, I'm fine! Mags and Luca are great, and everything's going good at school. People asked a bunch of questions at first, but they know I'm okay and you're a really good mom."

There's a long silence on the other end, and for a minute I worry the call has been dropped. Finally, Mom's voice comes back, small and brittle. "Make sure you do good in classes, so they see the bright, smart star you are, all right, pretty girl? Let them know the Malone girls are strong."

"You know I always do," I try to tease, licking tears off my lips. "And you better eat *your* carrots."

"If you eat your peas," she answers weakly. "I'd kill for some Bojangles. I love you, Magnolia Grace."

I almost shoot back my usual protest about my name being Sparrow, but this time I can't do it. It feels like the thread connecting us is more fragile, and I'm scared to do anything that might snap it.

"I love you, too, Mom."

After I give Mags her cell phone back, I excuse myself to my room. I can tell my aunt and uncle are worried—I probably would be, too, since my eyes are all puffy and red. They're nice enough not to ask the questions on their faces, though. Mags lets it pass with, "Missing someone can be so hard! We're here if you decide you'd like a hug or have questions."

But admitting I was rattled by Mom's call feels like treachery. One hug, and everything I'm feeling would pour out like water. I imagine Mom, sitting on the living room couch and hearing me say things like "My mom has a real problem, and it scares me" or "What if she doesn't get better, Mags?" Something important between the two of us would shatter.

So instead, I dive headlong into my homework for Monday. I blast some study music on my school laptop and power through ratios and vocabulary, channeling my feelings. It soothes me, being able to come up with the right answers—like I'm becoming less and less helpless with every completed page.

Finally, the only things left in the unfinished section of my homework folder are my garden project for science and the reflection monologue for drama. I write myself a note to ask Mags later if November and Azul can be my garden mentors, then doodle a big smiley face beside it.

Now, it's just me and the reflection monologue. I scan

the piddly paragraph I started last night and rip it from the notebook, balling it up. I write the title on a crisp new paper, where it hangs like a question, mocking me.

Sparrow's Truth

I blank for an eternity, clever words failing me. I'm annoyed I can't check out books on myself at the library or Google "interesting facts about Sparrow Malone." Twice, I even stop my fingers from navigating to the Tennessee Watchable Wildlife database on my school laptop out of habit. Because I'm not wild. I don't even feel interesting, really. I'm just Sparrow, terrified and trying to survive. I'm sure not turning *that* truth into a monologue.

Still, I need this grade desperately. Plus, Wynn and Sully are counting on me to do my bit before they can even start rehearsing and making costumes.

I growl, dramatically flopping onto my back on the floor. "Yowch, ugh!" Something hard pokes my shoulder blades, and I twist around and yank it out from under me. I'm ready to spite-chuck whatever it is across the room when I freeze, mouth gaping. It's one of my red boots.

The boots I'm 99.99999 percent certain I left on the rack by the front door last night.

"I'm loooosing it," I whimper in a singsong voice. My hand trembles as I gently settle my boot back on the carpet like it's a bomb that might detonate. As I do, something crinkles inside it. With a deep breath, I remove a white piece of paper with two fingers.

It's my list of Thou Shalt Nots—my pact with Shadow. A trade for a grade.

Okay, I think. *Touché.* Because boots magically transporting to my room or not, this is the deal we made. And being stuck on this reflection monologue for *two whole days* is the perfect moment for me to barter with Shadow for help.

"Here we go," I whisper. I slip on my boots and unfurl the crumpled list.

Shadow appears. It stares at me, pensive for a moment, then moves like it's coming in for a hug. I jump back, throwing out a hand.

"*WHOA*, weirdo. This is my space; that's yours. I'm here for bargains only."

Shadow shrinks back apologetically.

"So, the thing is, I need your luck for this drama

monologue on 'finding my truth.' If I do the next thing on the list, will you help me?" I point to the first item: *no beets*.

Shadow cocks its head like a praying mantis. Today, it's less black hole and more shimmering night sky, full of little sparks and crackles of light. It points to the top of the list, then slowly runs its finger down the entire length.

"The whole *thing*?" I choke in disbelief.

Shadow nods.

The room is suddenly hot and stuffy. I fan myself with my T-shirt, breathing hard. I can smell the dust in the sun-warmed carpet, and strands of hair stick to my sweaty neck.

"You can't be serious," I hiss finally, putting fingers to my braid. *Snip, snip, snip.* There are things on that list—huge things—that I couldn't hide from Mom if I wanted to. When I wrote them all out, I ordered them from smallest to biggest, assuming I'd never need to do the final items.

Shadow squats on the floor by my pitiful one-paragraph monologue assignment and strikes a dramatic pose, kicking one foot up in the air and shrugging.

"Nice. I see your point. The essay is huge, so it'll cost me the whole list, is that it?"

Shadow slow claps. Completely obnoxious.

I glare, half furious, half . . . something else. My eyes

rake the list, and a giddy bubbling dances beneath my ribs. I calculate this for a minute. *It's not because I'm excited*, I decide. It's just that excitement and anxiety are easy to confuse. They both involve the hormone adrenaline, according to my science textbook. Adrenaline gets your body ready to do something challenging, which would explain why I'm suddenly bouncing on the balls of my feet, feeling like I just drank an entire pot of Luca's strong coffee.

This is just a really big challenge. And I'm doing it for Mom.

"Time to get to work, then," I say to Shadow. Since the original Thou Shalt Not list is tattered, I copy it down into a sturdier notebook—except this time, there are zero "nos" to be seen. Mom's Thou Shalt Not rules are gone. This is a to-do list.

Chapter Nine
Sparrow Breaking Rules

Sparrow Malone

Ms. Ishihara

Science Homework, Fifth Grade

Report on Invertebrates

Some invertebrates, like insects, have exoskeletons. This means they grow a protective skeletal structure on the surface of their bodies rather than inside, in the form of a crunchy material called chiton. And while a mammal's bones grow as the animal grows, exoskeletons must be split, shed, and reformed as they're outgrown. The splitting and shedding process is called molting. In some areas in the world, you can find empty cicada exoskeletons all over the trees and ground during the summer when a whole brood molts.

Right after an insect sheds, it can take a while for the proteins that form their exoskeleton to get tough and solid again. A forest roach's shell can look transparent during this period, and the insect is softer and more vulnerable. But this splitting time also makes it capable of fantastic, unrestricted growth.

"Hey, Aunt Mags?"

"Hmmm?"

"Does the community garden have beets?"

Mags glances up from grading papers and grimaces. "Like the vegetable? No, I don't think so, love. They're a winter plant, so none right now. But I can put some on the grocery list if you like. I hate them myself, but I'm sure Luca has a recipe or two up his sleeve."

I nod. Beets will have to wait, I guess. Then, another

thought strikes me. If Mags and my mom dislike the same food, maybe it's because of something to do with Mom's past at Windy Hall before it became Rainbow House. Maybe I can cheat Shadow a little and ask Mags about Mom's past—another item on the List—and avoid pissing off Mom right now.

"Hey, Mags?"

"Yes, love?"

"*Why* don't you eat beets? Is it the same reason my mom doesn't?"

Mags raises her eyebrows. "Oh, probably so. We hated them as kids since we had the misfortune of eating them several times a week."

"Wait, seriously?" I blink. Several times a week is a lot, even for your favorite food. Mom and I have the running joke about carrots and peas, but it's sarcasm. We both gag on them. She's always gone out of her way to make sure I enjoy our meals. "Didn't your parents know you hated beets?"

"Some people think negative reinforcement can teach kids things. Personally, I find fear confuses my thinking more than it helps it. But my parents threatened us with our least-favorite foods hoping it would scare our brains into maturing faster, so we'd behave more like adults."

My face twists. That's the most illogical thing I've ever heard. It's just scientifically . . . *bonkers*. "Sooo, they fed you beets . . . because they thought it would magically . . . make you *older*," I say slowly.

Mags laughs. "You could put it that way. Magical beets, among harsher punishments."

I'm speechless. Mom's not perfect, but she never told me, "Little Maggie Grace, it's so annoying that you don't know how to do percentages yet. Eat this magic cucumber, then do my taxes."

That must have been confusing for a little kid, I think. It makes sense why Mom turns into a nervous wreck every time she mentions Windy Hall. *When she gets better, maybe we can visit Mags sometime. Then Mom can see how much it's changed*, I think. Then again, there might be plenty here that upsets her in new ways, too.

"Wynn came by again," Aunt Mags calls over her shoulder. She's moved to the stove, wrangling the whistling teakettle. "I have a suspicion she might keep popping by until you go say hello."

Maybe Wynn wants to do a sleepover, I think. Interrupting my usual nighttime routine makes me nervous, but it's one of the items on the List, so . . . "Is it okay if I go over?"

"Absolutely. So long as I'm up and awake, you're welcome to spend time at Wynn's."

"And could we do a sleepover sometime?" I press. "I don't really like staying over in new places. But maybe Wynn could come here?"

Mags beams. "That sounds lovely, Sparrow! I'm sure you and Wynn would have a blast. Let me and Luca tidy up today and rally some snacks. Does tonight suit?"

I grin. "Oh my god, yes! Thanks, Mags!" Before I lose my resolve, I dash over to Wynn's and rap on the glass door of her mobile home.

Wynn answers and squeals. "You're here!" She grabs my shoulders and yanks me inside. Her cozy house smells like brownies and popcorn. "I've died of boredom three times today already! Sully's off meeting one of his sisters for lunch, you were busy, and my dad is 'all peopled out' from teaching and needs to chill for a while,'" Wynn says, doing air quotes while I take off my shoes.

"But you're very welcome to have a friend over, Wynnie-the-Boo," a voice calls from the next room. "Hello, Sparrow!" I poke my head around the corner and see a handsome man with longish, curly blond hair seated in a wheelchair, drawing at an art easel while grooving to the music in his earbuds.

He looks really nice, but he also appears to be busy *in the zone*, sketching a fantastical elf-looking creature.

So I just wave shyly. Then Wynn drags me down the hall to her bedroom, a giant vat of pickles tucked under her other arm. Her room is almost exactly what I expected: art projects, graphic novels, severed doll parts, stacks of books . . .

I'm delighted to also spot a telescope, a microscope, and a giant cage with three napping ferrets all huddled in a heaving ball.

Wynn tosses me a throw pillow. "I hope you like pickles, 'cause Swedish ones are the best in the world. My grammy's recipe."

Before I can stop myself, I wrinkle my nose. "I don't eat cucumbers."

"Not a fan of gurka, huh? Don't worry. Grammy pickles anything that isn't nailed down. And she just visited, so we're *stocked*. What do you like? We've got herring, carrots, beets, string beans, radishes, babies . . ." Wynn jokes, trailing off.

"BEETS, PLEASE!" I say it with so much force, my voice cracks.

Wynn looks amused. "Wow, so you're a fan. Grammy would be proud."

"I've never actually had them before," I admit, sheepish. "I'm just . . . excited to try them, I guess."

Wynn studies me in mock seriousness, squinting and twizzling her eyebrows between her fingers. "Good, good. I knew I sensed a spirit of adventure in you. C'mon, then, brave Sparrow—*to the beets!*" Wynn points an imaginary sword and charges to the kitchen, and I follow her, a little self-conscious and laughing.

The pickled beet jar is full of sunshine-yellow orbs, floating in briny water with feathery herbs, peppercorns, and little star-shaped spices. "I thought beets were red," I observe as Wynn unscrews the jar.

"These are golden beets. Totally my favorite shade of yellow—almost like turmeric!" Wynn jabs a long fork into one of the vegetables and hands it to me, dripping.

"Just . . . bite it?" I ask, cringing as rivulets of pickle juice stream down the fork and onto my hand.

"Chomp chomp," Wynn says, grinning.

I hesitate. Mom has always described the taste of beets as sad, dirt-flavored rubber slices from a can, so I brace myself as I go in for the kill. *Here's to your health, Mom. Get better soon*, I think.

Sweet crunchiness fills my mouth—kind of like an apple, but with way more tang and spice. And, yeah, just a hint of dirt. I grin, eyes watering, and give a thumbs-up. It's super potent but not bad. Wynn cackles as juice drools down my chin, and she tosses me a napkin. I do a cool twirl and snatch it midair with my left hand, then take another bite. "Mmmmmm."

"Yeah?"

"Yeah, I like it! It's nice."

Wynn grins wider. "You need some water, don't you?"

"I do need water—yes, very much." I laugh, coughing.

I gulp from the glass Wynn hands me. Then I settle the remaining half beet on the counter before tugging my notebook and stubby pencil from my back jeans pocket. With a flourish, I strike out *beets*. I also cross out *bats* and *ask about M's past*, even though that last one is maybe a cheat since I asked Mags, not Mom.

"Um, hi, what's *this*?" Wynn asks, nosing into my space.

"It's uh—kind of like a bucket list. They're things I want to try in the next week."

"Weird stuff, haircut, ugly clothes . . ." Wynn reads, giggling. "You want to try ugly clothes?"

127

My face flares. "I phrased that wrong," I hedge. "I guess I meant . . . find clothes that are my style, even if some people would think they're ugly." *My mom, for instance.*

"Sparrow Malone," Wynn says solemnly, taking both my hands.

"Yes, 'Wynnie-the-Boo'?"

"Would you allow me to embark on this mysterious bucket-list journey with you, as your faithful companion and weirdness advisor?"

I blink, surprised. "You want to help?"

"Oh yeah! If it's weirdness and adventure you crave, I know all the best places to find it. I already have, like, twelve ideas. But only if you want the help."

I toe the edge of the cabinet. This is a very bad idea. Letting someone else—*anyone else*—in on my deal with Shadow, helping me trample Mom's unspoken rules, feels like letting them close to Mom and her problems. It would let Wynn closer to me, too, and I prefer keeping private—a *snob*, according to some of the meaner kids I've met. But as Wynn presses the backs of my hands with her soft, sunburn-peeling thumbs, I feel myself squeeze back.

Because she's my friend, I realize. And since she's my friend, I'm developing a big, kind-of-scary soft spot for her.

It's weird, having someone else share the tender place in my heart that usually only Mom occupies. Not like a crush. This is just as intense as how I feel about Kylie—maybe even more—but still, different. If Kylie's all electric zings and butterflies, Wynn reminds me more of how I feel about the first daffodil in spring. She's hopeful and brave and tender, and I suddenly realize I'd happily tackle whoever dares to mess with her. It surprises me, but I think I'm warming up to her offer to help me, too.

"Fine. Let's do it," I relent, smiling.

My turbo-brain goes back to stressing over what's next on the List. "How about we start tonight? Wanna sleep over at Mags's place?"

Wynn squeals. "Yes, yes, yes!!" She careens around the corner and shouts into the living room, "DAD, I'M SLEEPING OVER AT SPARROW'S!"

I poke my head around, too, to see Mr. Soderlund's response.

He shoots a thumbs-up. Then he pops out an earbud and pulls out his wallet, holding out a ten-dollar bill to Wynn. "In case y'all order pizza or something. Have fun, Boo-Bear!"

"C'mon," says Wynn. Her eyes are high beams of

determination. "Let's go pack my suitcase. Then we have to call and invite Sully."

"Wait, *Sully's* coming, too?"

"Is that okay? 'Cause I have a brilliant idea."

I shrug. Sully's my friend, too. "We'll have to ask Mags. Wait, did you just say you're packing a *suitcase*? Why? It's just one night."

Wynn wiggles her shoulders. "Oh, you'll see."

Chapter Ten
Sparrow Waking Up

Sparrow's notebook, age ten

I'm writing this here, because arguing with Mom
isn't okay. But she's W R O N G about something,
and I might bite someone if I don't say so. She keeps
saying possums are filthy and ugly and carry rabies,
but DIARY, listen: North American possums have
a lower body temperature than most mammals,
which makes it hard for them to host that virus. In
fact, it's super rare for them to catch rabies. Plus,
they clean themselves as well as cats do, and they

clean up carrion, too. Bonus cool fact: They're often immune to rattlesnake venom!

But mostly? It's my opinion that possums are extremely *good-looking*.

You know you've found a good pal when they listen to your info dumps without running for the hills. Case in point: Two seconds after Wynn kicks her shoes off inside Mags's trailer, my hands pour sweat and I accidentally launch into a breathless three-minute rant about orb weaving spiders. Who *does* that?

Me. When I talk about familiar, fascinating things, it helps me feel less like my world is careening off into space. Reliable facts about animals and science are a warm, soothing blanket for my gnarly thoughts and nerves—my ultimate chill pill.

And right now, I need one because Mom has always forbidden friends from coming over. Sometimes even Mom can't predict her own rough days, which makes her nervous to invite people inside our private lives. So having Wynn and Sully sleep over at Mags's trailer, even though it's not technically my home, feels bizarre.

Plus, as I remove my shoes at the door I realize that no boots means no Shadow. But if Shadow doesn't see me do the daring deeds on my list tonight, will they still count? All this is tumbling through my head while I show Wynn to my room.

My mouth is an unstoppable force.

". . . so it's good there are so many orb weavers around the garden, since they do insect control along with the little brown bats. They look dangerous, but they're completely harmless to humans. The yellow garden spider is my favorite." I pause to take a breath.

"Well"—Wynn grunts and heaves her massive suitcase onto my bed—"*I* like the ones with the red legs and the fierce black shoulder spikes, myself. Did you know that in Ukraine, Christmas trees are decorated with spiderwebs?"

I sigh in relief, smiling. Wynn apparently gets my need to nerd out about things, and I don't have to apologize for it. "No way, seriously?"

"So, legend goes, there was a mother who didn't have money to decorate her Christmas tree for her children. They all went to bed crying, and the spiders heard them. Then, in the middle of the night, the spiders crawled onto the tree and covered it with dozens of gossamer webs," Wynn recites.

The story tugs at my heart—maybe because it reminds me of the Christmas in Alabama when it snowed so much, it didn't matter that I only got itchy ruffled dresses for presents because Mom and I spent the whole day sledding on cardboard boxes together. But I change the subject instead of sharing this with Wynn.

"So, you crammed half your closet into that mammoth suitcase, and I'm dying to know why."

"Wait till Sully gets here!" Wynn sings, swinging her feet as she perches on the edge of my bed. She's beaming like an imp, which makes her round cheeks look less cherubic and more . . . adorably sinister.

Soon the doorbell rings, sending Bela Pugosi into his usual spasms.

Sully lugs an enormous duffel bag—a dance bag, I think—and it's absolutely overstuffed to the point of explosion. "So tell me about this list," he says in a teasing voice.

"*Wynn!*" I protest. "You told him?"

"Sorry! But how else are we supposed to help you fulfill your wildest dreams?"

I shake my head in feigned exasperation. Wynn and Sully seem to be a package deal, so telling one is basically the same as telling the other. As for "wildest dreams," it dawns on me that a couple items actually are wild dreams of mine, including this sleepover. I squash a flicker of guilt.

"Bags. What's in them?! Tell!"

Wynn's fingers splay in excitement. "Okay, so, every Saturday night, Sully and I video chat while we watch our favorite alternative drag show."

"Your favorite whaty-what-what?"

A long look passes between Sully and Wynn. It's brimming with wordless best-friend shorthand. I gnaw my thumbnail, partly because I feel left out and partly because I know this exchange is about me. "Y'all? Say something please?"

Sully clears his throat. "Okay so, *drag*. You know what that is, right?"

I hate talking about stuff I'm not already an expert in. I sweat from being put on the spot. "Kind of? It's . . . when men wear makeup and dresses for shows, right?" My stretching mind tries to get more specific: Not like Aunt Mags—Mags *is* a woman, but one I've never seen wear a dress, come to think of it. And not like Sully, who's a guy who does wear dresses in his everyday life.

Sully clasps his hands. "Sort of. Drag is when people try on gender expressions, often different from the one they live in—"

"But not always!" Wynn interjects.

"—*but not always!* In an exaggerated way, kind of as art. And as a way to have fun together or make a bigger point about how our culture defines gender."

"There can be drag queens, drag *kings*, and personas that are neither," Wynn adds.

"Okay," I say, starting to get it, "so you make up a persona different than your everyday one, and then you perform it. I already knew about drag queens, kind of." I don't admit I've never actually seen a performance, not even on TV. "And drag kings . . . are exaggerated guy characters?"

"Exactly!" Sully says.

"Alternative drag can be kings, queens, or neither— but with some horror, monsters, or fantasy elements mixed in! Like on our favorite show, *Monster of the Week*," Wynn gushes. "It's a way for queer people to express themselves. And it's *awesome*."

I flinch at the word *queer*. I've heard Mom use it a few times, but she says it like it's a bad thing. Like it's embarrassing? She slips into a harder tone, too, like she's parroting someone meaner who says it that way.

Mom wore the same strained look when I told her I wanted to marry my teacher, Miss Jasmine, when I was in second grade. Privately, I don't feel embarrassed for liking girls, and I know it's normal enough—I don't live under a rock, even if Mom wishes we could. Still, I don't ever bring it up around her. I like the occasional boy, too. But do I get to call myself "queer," then? Who gets to say it?

My stomach squirms as I imagine how she'd react to this drag conversation.

If my deal with Shadow is going to work, I have to give myself permission to stop worrying about that, I realize. I press on.

"So . . ." I point at their bags.

Wynn bounces in excitement. "They're full of costume supplies! We're gonna have so much fun!"

Sully explains in more detail. "Okay, so, creating a drag persona can help you learn things about your sense of style. And *Monster* is all about embracing your inner uniqueness—"

"That's two things from your bucket list, Sparrow—sleepover *and* new style!" Wynn interjects. "Sorry—go on, Sully."

". . . so Wynn suggested we watch episodes while we all design our own monster drag characters," Sully finishes.

"FASHION SHOW!" Wynn yells, twirling.

I smile but feel slightly queasy. I'm good at pretending to be someone else, at morphing into what people expect.

But expressing my "inner weirdo"? I swallow hard. I don't like expressing my inner *anything*.

Sully is already carefully unloading his dance bag: There are stacks of drawing pencils, sketch pads, a few wigs, a tackle box full of makeup, and several sets of rubber pointed ears, all nicely arranged on my bed. Meanwhile, Wynn hums while she clicks open her suitcase and upends its contents all over my floor. Fabric in every hue of the rainbow spills across the carpet.

Wynn opens her laptop on my dresser and starts an episode of *Monster of the Week*. From the moment the spooky, thumping theme music plays, I'm hooked. I sink onto Wynn's pile of fabric, cupping my chin in my hands, eyes glued to the screen.

Each episode, the contestants design a new drag monster persona for that night's competition. They represent many body shapes, backgrounds, and cultures, I notice. Each person is an incredible artist. I gaze, slack-jawed, as they use makeup, costume, and acting to transform themselves into a character that expresses something about them.

After a couple of episodes, Sully scoots beside me and hands me a notepad. "Time to work!"

I glance at the notebook on his lap. He's sketched a

whimsical character with fangs and pointed ears. Wynn's already at work behind us, using safety pins to shape brown fuzzy fabric into a pair of giant wings.

"I have no clue what I'm doing," I mutter. My hearing starts to do its muffled, garbled thing. *I'll be so awkward, and then I'll die from embarrassment*, I think. I focus on breathing in-two-three-four, out-two-three-four.

After a minute, Sully taps my elbow gently with the back of his finger. "You okay?"

"I'm just drawing a blank here," I croak.

Wynn squats beside us. "Aw, Sparrow, we don't have to do this. We can just listen to music or something."

"*No,*" I shoot back stubbornly. And maybe a little too loudly. I need to figure this out, though—it's on the List. "I just have to brainstorm."

"That's cool. Let's think." Wynn screws up her face. "You know how some contestants on *Monster of the Week* are inspired by characters like Red Riding Hood or Medusa?"

I nod.

"Pick a character you've always loved and make it yours. Don't think so hard. How about your favorite monster?"

I gasp as the answer literally floats to the top of my mind. Ever since I saw *Creature from the Black Lagoon* on TV once, I get a bittersweet ache in my chest whenever I think of the underwater scene where the fish monster swims around, mesmerized by the humans that have invaded his home. He always seemed so lonely to me. Like someone on the outside of a window, looking in, trying to understand what it means to be alive when you don't match anyone around you. He means . . . *something* to me, even if I'm not sure what.

"Okay, wow," I say, grinning. "Wynn, that worked."

"I know," Wynn says, preening. "I'm brilliant."

"Hey, Sully, can I borrow some makeup?" I ask. I suddenly wish I felt comfortable bumping my head on his shoulder, which surprises me.

The corners of Sully's eyes crinkle with a smile. "Yesss, Sparrow! But not my mascara. We don't want anyone getting pink eye."

Just for the record, makeup is hard, and the people who are good at it are wizards. I'm glad I don't wear it every day. I've always been curious, but after this, I'm certain it's not for me—way too goopy. Still, just for tonight, I love the results.

With a lot of sketching and some help from Sully, my face transforms into a greenish monster with little scales around the edges. Dark shading makes my jaw look strong and my face look more angular, and I almost don't recognize myself in the mirror. My stomach does the same little dance it did the first time I saw myself in my boots—like I just learned something new and important, even though I can't put my finger on it.

Wynn twists my hair up so it looks like a red fin on the top of my head, and I drape a seaweed-colored cloak around me to complete the look.

I feel . . . well, there's certainly nothing recognizable as Magnolia Grace here. It's more like I could be *anybody*—like Halloween, but better. Because this is a persona I created for me, just for fun. I find myself asking Mags to take a picture of the three of us so I can always remember this.

Wynn has transformed into "Moth Ma'am," complete with red heels, enormous eyelashes, and a curly black pipe cleaner proboscis I made for her. Sully is a vegetarian vampire with a fruit-print cape and pointed ears, somehow managing to look elegant and graceful even with modeling-clay fangs. I help them clean up their supplies, then the three of us goof off for the camera, and I find myself prancing and posturing in ways I could never do without being "Monsieur Lagoon."

By the time we wash our faces and clean up, my eyes burn from makeup and exhaustion. Mags hauls sleeping bags into the living room, plus a night-light. Sully and Wynn are snoring softly by the time I grab my notebook with the List, to cross out today's items.

"Sleepover, done."

I want to cross out "wear my own style," too, because I think I'm getting closer to understanding what I like. I like looking strong and neat—nothing too extra. And I love feeling cozy. The simple green cloak tonight felt nice.

It might feel perfect if I could remind people of a strong, happy Bob Ross tree. Like how I feel when Luca's doing the dishes in his rolled-up old man sleeves, whistling while he smells like pine-needle cologne. Or sometimes the way Teacher Jones looks in vests or colorful bow ties. Dapper? Cute-but-not-pretty? Handsome, but in a fancy way? I don't even begin to know where to find clothes like those for myself. *Why is this so hard?*

I cross out "wear my own style" but only halfway. After all this thinking, I feel like I deserve partial credit. I'll try to finish the rest of it tomorrow.

I can't sleep. So I pull out my school laptop and do what

I do best: learn every fact I can about a new topic until I feel more competent.

I'm curious about how drag started, and soon I learn that the first queen of drag was a Black man named William Dorsey Swann, 130 years ago, right after the Civil War. People treated him horribly, not only because of their bigotry, but also because he was gay and held drag balls in his home. *That's a lot of unfair, stacked on even more awful unfairness*, I think. My fists ball up and tears sting my nose. I scroll across old black-and-white photographs of beautiful queens like William. They all look stunning in their old-fashioned dresses and bonnets, posing and grinning just like Sully, Wynn, and I were earlier tonight.

I'm lucky, I realize. Mags and Luca wouldn't bat an eye if I said I was . . . *queer*—not that I'm volunteering. I have Sully and Wynn, too, and whole reality shows full of people who seem like my kind of weird, thanks to William Dorsey Swann. Which sends me into a whirlwind of searching for information about all my favorite *Monster of the Week* contestants, because I'm so curious about what their lives are like outside the show.

I click and read for half an hour until something catches

my eye. I lean closer to the screen, barely breathing. One of my favorite contestants, Sedge Birdsong, uses they and them pronouns, just like November. I scroll. Under the gender identity part of their info is the word *nonbinary*.

Everyone's sound asleep, but I check to make sure no one's watching anyway before typing "what does nonbinary mean" into the search bar. Holy bananas, there are a lot of answers. There are websites and infographics and articles filled with different definitions and opinions of what it means to be nonbinary—plus some people just being plain rude.

But after almost an hour of skimming, I decide the main idea seems to be that nonbinary people are those who don't fit neatly into either gender category of "boy" or "girl." Binary means one thing or the other, after all. Nonbinary means not being "man" or "woman," because neither one fits.

Neither. Both. Something else.

I softly close the laptop and curl on top of my sleeping bag, my heart thumping as fast as any bird's. I don't say it out loud, just silently mouth the syllables, almost like I'm praying them. The word feels like a precious wish, and if I spoke it, reality would come snatch it right from my lips and

then my heart would break. Because I know I could never—
Because Mom. Because . . .

Tonight, words are thieves. I don't want them to steal this glowing feeling from my ribs.

So instead, I curl around the precious ember in the dark of Mags's living room and shield it. I'll keep it quiet and close and secret. *Neither. Both. Something else.*

Chapter Eleven
Sparrow Branching Out

Sparrow Malone

Miss Thibodeaux

Science Homework, Fourth Grade

Environmental Adaptation and the Deep Sea

My favorite animal is a fish called a blob sculpin. You might know it as simply "blobfish." Some people think this fish is the ugliest animal in the world, but that's only because they've never seen it in its natural environment. It has specialized bones and tissue that are capable of living at 9,000 feet beneath the ocean's surface where there is lots of pressure.

Down there, the blob sculpin is actually cute! It's only when people haul them up to the lower-pressure surface that their jelly body expands into a gooey mess. So, I think it's not fair to judge them too harshly.

The next morning, everyone is still wiped out, so Sully and Wynn go home to sleep in their own beds around eight. I yawn and stretch, wishing I could nap, too. But a quick glance at my assignment calendar tells me I should tackle the next item on the List, so I sneak a cup of coffee instead. Sully and Wynn have been nice enough not to ask how my drama monologue's going. But I know it must be on their minds, since the group project is due in just two weeks.

I need to start my extra credit garden project for Mr. Fullilove's science class, too. And even though it's still hotter than Hades outside in late August, there's only a handful of weeks left before fall. That doesn't leave much growing season left for my project.

That makes "weirdos" (aka my new garden mentors, November and Azul) the perfect next List item to tackle, I decide.

Besides that, I can't stop carrying my secret wish around in my head like a sputtering flame. *Neither. Both. Something else.* Part of me hopes just being around November—and finding out if they're nonbinary—will give me clues to understanding these jumbled feelings.

Mags is outside on the dewy grass letting Bela do his business, so I tie on my boots, wave a good morning to Shadow, and run out to talk to her.

"Hey, Aunt Mags? Is it okay if Azul and November supervise my garden project?"

"Oh, you met them—how wonderful! I think that's a great idea."

Mags points to the little open-air pavilion on the other side of the garden, just across from Rainbow House. "If I had to guess, Azul and November are up there helping Teacher Rose—that's our garden manager."

My Shadow is already tearing across the garden, so I call "Thanks, Mags!" and chase after it. I want Shadow to slow down and check in with me first so I can fill it in on last night's success, but it's too fast. I'm sweaty and gulping air before I know it, dodging bean trellises and climbing over squash vines trying to catch it.

Shadow skids to a halt at the pavilion and waves for me

to hurry up. A little group of people has gathered, some holding five-gallon buckets and others, fancy baskets. November and Azul are there, chuckling as a white-haired Asian lady in a long-sleeved denim shirt and glasses cracks a joke while pointing out at the woods that edge the garden. Shadow edges closer to the group, so I follow along.

"Oh, hey, Sparrow!" Azul spots me and waves me over. "We're doing our community hours," she whispers. "Blackberry-picking day. Teacher Rose is reminding us about ticks and which snakes to watch out for. Wanna help?"

"Seriously? *Yeah!*"

"I strongly suggest wearing a long-sleeved shirt, unless you enjoy looking like you've been bathing feral cats," Teacher Rose is saying. "These brambles are very thick and full of thorns. I also suggest nice, sturdy boots, since we're venturing into the undergrowth. Rattlesnakes and copperheads don't want to bite you, but they won't hesitate to if they're startled."

November glances over at my outfit. I'm wearing my long-sleeved Wolverine sweatshirt—even though the August air feels like hot soup, it's still my favorite—and my red work boots. November nods and shoots me a thumbs-up. "Good to see you, buddy!"

My heart skips at the way November calls me "buddy."

When Teacher Rose is done giving instructions, November and Azul introduce me, and I let her know they'll be supervising me. She smiles and welcomes me, and then we're off to the edge of the property.

Shadow cartwheels and dances across the grass and clover, but once we reach the brambles, it freezes beside me. For once, it mirrors me the way it's supposed to, standing with hands clasped against its chest, staring at the thicket. White flowers, bobbing with bees and wasps, swirl together with black berries and electric-pink ones that aren't ripe yet. Down on the ground, ants swarm the overripe fruits that have fallen.

"They're pretty, right?" Azul says, handing me a bucket.

I nod. I know a lot about nature, to the point that I'm practically an expert on certain animals and biomes. But I don't actually spend a ton of time outside. This is as soothing as my library books but in a whole different way.

"First time picking, Sparrow?" November asks.

I think about lying to impress them, but Shadow wags a finger. "Yeah," I admit. "First time."

"Hey, that's exciting! So, we're looking for the berries that are totally dark and come off the vines easily," November says, demonstrating. With deft motions, they pluck a handful of berries and plop them into their bucket. "You try!"

I accidentally squish one or two, but soon I've got the hang of it, and my bucket's halfway full. Every so often, I pop a few in my mouth and savor their sweetness, until my teeth are full of blackberry pips.

"So how are you liking Brightbarrel?" Azul asks. "Make any friends yet?"

I grin a little shyly, then tell Azul and November about Sully and Wynn, and the fun we had last night.

"I think I've heard of *Monster of the Week*! I don't get to watch much TV since college, though." Azul laughs, taking off her glasses to wipe away beads of sweat.

"And I have a hard time sitting still," November grunts, jumping to grab a low tree branch and swinging on it.

"Ants in their pants, *all the time*," Azul says with a smirk.

I'm a little disappointed because I hoped *Monster of the Week* would start a conversation about . . . *things*. Shadow pokes me. *"Stop it,"* I mouth. Shadow pokes me again, and I fight the urge to turn around and throw a punch. *Fine.*

"So, um. One of the contestants on *Monster* also uses they and them pronouns like you do, November."

November and Azul exchange a glance. "Yeah? So what'd you think about that?" November asks.

"Their webpage says they're nonbinary, I guess?" *Why did you make me bring this up?* I mentally screech at Shadow. My stomach is busy trying to earn its Girl Scouts KNOTS badge, and I think I might hurl all the blackberries I just ate.

"Are you . . . wondering if I'm nonbinary, too?" November asks, a little grin in their voice.

I don't look at them. Instead, I focus hard on reaching a particular blackberry. But I nod while I do it, because I really want to know.

"I'm nonbinary!" November shouts into the sky, like it's a war cry. Azul face-palms, and I can't help but giggle.

"It took me a little while to figure it out," November goes on more seriously. "When I was a kid, no one explained to me that there were different ways to be. I was so confused, but it wasn't because I didn't understand myself. More like . . . I didn't have words to explain myself. Does that make sense? Like, imagine trying to explain the color green to someone if you didn't know the name for it!"

It makes perfect sense, I think. Because I have feelings— a whole lot of them, swarming and changing shape like a murmuration of starlings, and I'm not sure how to explain them, either. "But nonbinary fit?"

November nods and shows me a little pin on their hat. It's a flag with yellow, white, purple, and black stripes. "See? The nonbinary pride flag. My brother gave it to me for my birthday."

I swallow hard. "So your family . . . understands about it?"

"My brother does. And so does my grandma. Everyone else is a work in progress." November still smiles, but the muscles around their eyes strain a little. *That makes them sad*, I realize. I feel bad about asking and try to change the subject fast.

"How about you, Azul? Do you have a flag?"

Azul throws back her head and cackles. "Well, the rainbow flag is good. But if we're talking about gender, my flag would be, like, an invisibility cloak." She throws an arm up like she's hiding behind a cape, Count Dracula–style. "*Do not perceive me! My gender is 'meh,' but 'she' and 'her' pronouns work.*" She laughs.

I'm stunned. I didn't realize there were *options* like that. And suddenly, I'm maybe more confused than ever. *Hey, Distracty McGee, focus!* my brain orders. *You have grades to fix.*

"I'm not sure what I want to do for my garden project yet," I announce. "Are there any plants that grow in, like, two weeks?"

Azul winces. "I don't think anything grows that fast. Some seeds take that long just to germinate."

My heart sinks. I don't have months. The longer Mom's in a tailspin, the tougher it is to pull her out.

"You know what might work, though?" November says suddenly. "It's not start-to-finish growing, but it would put you in charge of lots of plants at once! Mr. Hodges, one of the plot tenders, had to go into the hospital unexpectedly, and his plot is orphaned. We've all been taking turns with it, but what if we put Sparrow in charge?"

"Ayyy, that could be perfect!" Azul says. "You could call it 'Adopt-a-plot'! What do you think, Sparrow? Feel like you can learn how to do tomatoes, beans, and flowers all at once?"

I nod, grinning.

"Okay. Every afternoon for an hour right after school, meet us at plot number forty-five. It's the one with all the pinwheels."

A little while later, I race back to the trailer to cross "weirdos" off in my notebook, when a Jeep rolls down the gravel driveway. Sully sits in the passenger seat, and a stylish young lady is driving.

"Hey!" I wave. "Back so soon?"

"Someone left his pillow behind." The young woman laughs. "You must be Sparrow! I'm Leah, Sullivan's sister. We're just swinging by to grab a couple of things he left last night."

"Then we're going clothes shopping," Sully shouts from the passenger seat. He shoots me a meaningful look. "Wanna come with?"

My first impulse is to gag and say no thanks. But as I start to, Sully mouths, *Your bucket list!* Oh. *Right.* I grit my teeth and pretend to look excited, glancing at Sully's big sister for the okay.

Leah lowers her sunglasses and gives an easy smile. "If you want to, Sparrow, and if your auntie says it's fine, we'd love to have you come with us."

Aunt Mags gives me the okay (after checking my scalp for ticks) and palms me several twenty-dollar bills. "My treat. Get some new jeans!" My eyes bug, but Mags insists, laughing as she pecks me on the cheek and tells me to have a good time. I decide to never tell my mom about the money—she'd think it was charity, even though I know it's just Mags being Mags.

Leah's Jeep smells nice, like vanilla, and she stops and gets us drinks at a drive-through before we head to Trader Jolene's—Sully's idea. Shadow swirls with color, like a mysterious rainbow-colored nebula. It watches Sully and me thoughtfully as we swing out of the car onto the sidewalk, racing to see who gets to the front door first.

"Store manners, now, y'all," Leah reminds us as we enter the co-op. Sully and I squelch our giggles and stop running. I drop one of my twenty-dollar bills in the donation box, because it just feels right. Then the smell of fabric softener hits me, and suddenly I feel a little dizzy.

"I'll just follow you first," I tell Sully.

He nods, and soon he's eyeing fabrics and patterns critically. He walks his long fingers over the hangers, his dark eyes darting back and forth until—every now and then—they light up and sparkle because he finds something that's just right.

"Mmmhmm," he hums, yanking out a button shirt with tiny roses on it. "You're coming home with me!"

"How do you *know*?" I blurt.

"Know what?"

"That it's perfect. Like, how do you know it's what you want?"

Sully looks perplexed. "How do you know you love cherry soda?" he asks slowly. "You just know. See this?" He gently shakes the lightweight shirt, so it ripples. "It's swishy. Swishy is good. It moves like it's underwater, like me. We match. I like that. And I look *good* in orange." He holds it up to his face, and he's right. His warm brown skin springs to life, and his eyes sparkle. *Oh yeah*, I decide firmly. *My friend is definitely some kind of wizard.*

"I bet you look good in navy, Sparrow," Leah calls across a rack. I raise my eyebrows and blush a little.

"Yeah? How do you know?"

"Leah's an artist." Sully laughs. "Trust me. You should listen."

I try to look through the clothes myself, and instantly my shoulders knot. Dozens of past trips to fitting rooms are flashing through my mind—feeling like I was wearing someone else's clothes, someone else's body, someone else's life. I can recall Mom's voice praising me while I model some dress, but her encouragement bounced right off me. Like I wasn't really there.

The walls start to feel too close, and I feel sweat trickle down the middle of my back as I stare down a pink cardigan like it's my nemesis. "You okay, Sparrow?" Leah asks, frowning in concern.

"I just . . . can't find anything I like here." Nothing fits that comfortable, almost handsome feeling I had with my Monsieur Lagoon cloak last night. Not even close.

"Let's go over there, then," Sully says, shrugging. "I want to look for a tie anyway."

I freeze, stomach flipping. He's pointing to the boys and men's section. Can I just *do* that? I feel an electric buzz in my palm and look down to see Shadow's hand entwined with mine. It gives a gentle tug. *Come on*, it seems to say.

I set my jaw. Okay. That's why I'm here anyway, right? To convince Shadow to help me with Mom. I follow Sully.

Except I'm still overwhelmed, and I don't know where to start.

I need new jeans, I remind myself. It seems impossible, but I've grown several inches in the past couple of weeks. I breathe in and out slowly, searching until I find the sizes that look like they'd fit. I spot a pair that are the color of wet asphalt—not too tight, not too fancy, and just a little tough looking. But soft, too. A little self-conscious, I gather them to my chest and hug them like a safety blanket as I keep browsing.

Shadow starts thrusting its hand from inside one of the clothing racks like some demon from a pocket dimension, waving me over. It's creepy but weirdly very efficient. Every time Shadow flags me down, I find something that makes me go fizzy inside: a button-down shirt with dinosaurs, a soft navy hoodie, cozy flannel shirts, and a few boxy T-shirts with animals and trees screen-printed across the front.

Sully heads to the fitting rooms, and I follow, heart thumping.

Inside, I get dressed and stare for a minute, wide-eyed. The jeans fit just right over the tops of my red boots, and the button-down and hoodie coordinate perfectly—not too tight across my chest. Slowly, I blush, because dang, I'm really, *really* cute. Shadow hovers just behind me—probably feeding off this rule-breaking energy. I put my hand to the mirror and touch my reflection, lifting my jaw to study myself.

Then, I don't really know where my tears are coming from, or how to make them stop, but they're pouring down my freckled neck and into my new shirt in twin rivers.

I just know this feels really nice. I'm *here*, and not being tormented by that itchy-tag sensation of feeling like a stranger in someone else's clothes. And I'm heartbroken that I'll have to give this up when Mom gets out again. Because I'll totally have to stop wearing this new stuff. The boyishness of these outfits is a bridge further than her anxiety can tolerate, and I know that.

But it's worth it, right?

My hands move to pretend-haircut myself, self-soothing. *Snip, snip, snip.* Just for a second, I hold my hair up so it looks shorter, like November's. *Neither. Both. Something else.* The thought sends goose bumps up and down my arms and legs. "Hey in there, Sparrow," I whisper to the mirror.

"Hey in there, Sparrow!" I jump at Sully's voice outside the door. "You okay?"

I swipe the back of my hand over my cheeks, drawing a ragged breath. "Yeah! Everything works! Coming out soon!" I decide to wear my new outfit out of the store, without even washing it. Which I know is kind of gross, but if I only have a little while to enjoy these clothes, I want to make every second count. Hopefully, I won't be able to enjoy them for long because that means Mom is getting better fast.

And I want Mom back more than anything. I do. But now part of me is mad at Shadow for making it hurt so much.

Chapter Twelve
Sparrow, All Mixed Up

Sparrow's notebook, age nine

Mom says clothes say something about the sort of people we are, and that we shouldn't advertise the wrong thing, or we'll attract the wrong folks. What does that even mean? And how can I advertise that I'd like for people to mind their dang business and let me catch lizards? If my clothes could make mean people leave me alone, I think I'd like that fine. Especially our hateful old neighbor, Mrs. Sims. It might be even better if Mom would take my side, for once.

The first few days of the school week blur by as I hustle my way through homework, shamelessly sucking up to my teachers, and learning the ropes with November and Azul in my adopted garden plot.

November stays patient as I accidentally overwater the tomatoes a few times, causing the fruit to expand too quickly and split. "It's all right"—they say, grinning—"you can still eat the ugly ones." Azul gently chides me for being in a rush as I pull the weeds on Wednesday, accidentally yanking up several zinnia stalks in the process.

The highlights of my days are sitting next to Kylie in math class and doing silly drawings on each other's paper margins while we do our daily work. My favorite moment happens when we both run out of margins, and Kylie calmly reaches over and encircles my wrist with her cool fingers like a bracelet. She flips my arm over to draw on it instead. My heart skitters as the tickle of her felt-tipped marker creates a strawberry person with a petulant face on my skin, captioned "Exponents aren't my jam!" By the time math class is over, my right arm and Kylie's left are covered in doodles. My stomach fills with butterflies, and I wish I didn't have to wash the ink off later.

I don't see Kylie much at lunch, though, because her table is always jammed full of friends from church and her swim team. Which is fine by me, since I'm just as happy to eat with Sully—and a lot less self-conscious. Then every day after lunch, it's only a couple more classes until drama with both Sully and Wynn, and an hour in the garden, after which Wynn and I hang out in the evenings at her house, playing video games and doing homework. It's a nice rhythm.

Things start going sideways on Thursday. I stayed up late the night before, searching the internet for information about gender, and discovering that the scrambled, itchy-tag-in-my-soul feeling I get sometimes from certain clothes or being called "pretty girl" has a name: gender dysphoria. On the one hand, I feel better knowing it's not just me being weird. On the other hand, this makes me nervous, because naming it makes it feel less like a silly nothing that might just go away someday. *But what can I do about it?*

When I show up at school, I'm already on edge—Teacher Jones assigned two pages of math homework, and somehow, I left my book in my desk and I totally forgot to copy the examples up on the board. Azul tried her best to help me yesterday afternoon, but I kept nodding like I understood when really I didn't, because I didn't want her to know I was struggling.

So today, I'm walking into class early, knowing half my problems are wrong.

"It's going to be okay," Wynn says. "Teacher Jones is so chill, you can totally ask for help." She's walking me to class because I freaked out about it on the bus, and she's worried about me. Today, her face is covered in dozens of foil star stickers, and she's casually sipping water from a hollowed-out bell pepper with googly eyes on it. I don't ask why; I'm too nervous to listen. Wynn crosses her eyes at me, trying to make me laugh.

It works, for a second. "I'm just having an off day," I say. "I don't need to bother him."

"Sparrow, SEEK HELP!" Wynn yells, laughing. "That's what teachers are there for!"

My face flames as the principal walks by, frowning at the noise we're making in the hallway. "Make your way to class, ladies," she says. "It's almost bell."

I'm not a lady, I think. My fists ball up, and I feel my face go cranky.

Just then, Kylie arrives at the class door. Wynn is still clowning, trying to get me to loosen up, and accidentally spills water right in front of Kylie's white sneakers. Kylie shoots me a *look*, then rolls her eyes at Wynn. *"Excuse* me." As she pushes by Wynn, Kylie leans in close to my ear, brushing my arms with her fingertips. "Blink twice if you need to be rescued, okay? Wynn can be *a lot*."

I'm stunned for a second—Wynn's unconventional for sure, but that's why I like her. I'm surprised by Kylie's harsh warning. I don't know what to do, so I clamp my mouth and nod, hoping Wynn didn't hear Kylie's comment.

"What did she say?" Wynn whispers, eyebrows lowering.

"Nothing, just something about homework," I lie. "See you later, okay?"

Wynn frowns. "Okay, see ya."

I scuttle past Teacher Jones's desk, but he calls after me. "Sparrow! Everything fine? Things looked kinda tense in the hallway."

"Yeah, we were just messing around," I hedge. *Not smart, Sparrow. Turning in only half your homework already makes you look like a goof-off.* "Wynn was being kinda loud," I add.

My stomach churns. *You're getting strong from all that gardening*, I tell myself. *'Cause it took some serious muscle to toss Wynn under the bus like that.* I don't love how I'm handling this, but I don't know what else to do.

"Well, if you ever need help navigating something, please feel free to talk to me," Teacher Jones says. I nod and meekly hand in my half-wrong homework.

I slide into my seat, and Kylie shoots me a look. "You okay?"

I gulp and nod. "Fine. Just had a rough morning."

"Good. Wynn can be so loud sometimes, and hanging around her can get you into all kinds of trouble with teachers. Ask me how I know," she says, blowing her bangs.

I don't ask, just nod and look away.

Behind Kylie, Shadow is giving her devil horns with its fingers. I don't know that I agree with Shadow, though. I think Kylie's just trying to look out for me, same as Wynn, just in a different way.

"I bombed this homework," Kylie whispers.

"Same," I admit. Kylie looks a little surprised, then leans over and squeezes my hand.

"Want to come over to my house today and study? My mom picks me up after school, and you could ride with us."

Kylie gazes at me, doe eyes hopeful. *She's exactly the kind of girl Mom always wants me to be,* I think. Except I don't want to be her, I just want to be near her. Mom would probably love that, too, if she didn't know about my mammoth crush. There's a hidden gentle side to Kylie that makes me feel impossibly soft, almost to the point that it doesn't feel fair. She could probably ask me to do anything for her, no matter how risky, and I'd try it to make her smile—scale Mount Kilimanjaro, wrestle a badger, punch the sun . . .

"I'll have to call my aunt Mags," I murmur.

"You can use my cell in the bathroom after class." Kylie grins, beaming with delight. Teacher Jones gives us a stern throat-clearing noise, then whirls back to the dry-erase board.

"This is gonna be awesome," Kylie mouths. She reaches over and brushes a strand of my hair away from my face with her fingertips, then turns back to her paper.

My heart warms and expands like a marshmallow chick in a microwave.

I couldn't get Mags on the phone, so I left her a message saying I was riding to Kylie's. I figure that's probably fine, since she had no problem with me going to Wynn's or shopping with Sully's sister. Halfway to Kylie's house, though, I realize with a sinking feeling that I'm missing my mentoring in the garden. And Wynn is probably flipping out, wondering why I'm not on the bus, because I forgot to tell her.

It's easily the hottest day of the year out, but Kylie's

mom's AC blasts ice-cold air across the SUV's leather seats until my arms sprout chill bumps. I press my leg into Kylie's for warmth.

Mrs. Funquist swivels in her seat to study me before she cranks the car. "Well, Sparrow, honey, did you run out of clean laundry?"

"Nooo?" I glance down at my clean T-shirt and jeans. My face must be twisting in a funny way, because Kylie's mom chuckles.

"I suppose your *aunt*"—she overemphasizes the word for no apparent reason and makes her eyes go big like she's talking to a baby—"is the sort who'd let you pick out your own clothes."

My polite smile doesn't manage to iron out the wrinkles on my forehead. What Mrs. Funquist said about Mags letting me pick my own things is true, but somehow it doesn't feel compliment-y.

After a while, I decide Kylie's mom reminds me of mine, in a way, because she grills Kylie about school and fusses over her "disheveled" hair the rest of the way home. Mrs. Funquist is less anxious than Mom, though, and lots bossier. Her subtly highlighted hair looks . . . expensive. When her gray eyes scour me again from stem to stern as I exit the car,

I squirm. Shadow throws her a rude gesture. I'm eager to kick off my boots—"Careful not to scuff the wainscoting with those *work boots*, dear!"—and escape to Kylie's room.

Kylie's house isn't old and grand like Rainbow House, but it's much bigger and much fancier than Mags's trailer. The inside looks like a decorator magazine.

We work on homework for a while, then decide to take a break.

"So, how *are* you?" Kylie asks, flopping on her belly beside me on the bed. Her eyes probe into mine. Having her this close to me is making my head feel weird, and I blush under the attention.

"What do you mean?"

"You know. Your mom is sick in the hospital, so you had to go stay at the Rainbow Farm. My mom says they're all a bunch of hippies and wackos."

My mom, too, I think. I feel myself splitting almost in two—because I can understand what Kylie means. The people at Rainbow House are different. Most of me adores them for it. But another part, the part that belongs with Mom, knows she won't be thrilled if she ever sees where I've been staying.

"It's different, for sure," I say, because that feels neutral. It hurts my stomach to speak badly of Mags and Luca, Wynn and her dad, and November and Azul. They're my friends. But another part of me feels relieved to know Mom would approve of this conversation. I end up feeling guilty, all the way around.

"I knew you were just like me the minute I saw you." Kylie laughs. "I bet your mom is kind of strict, too."

"Yeah," I admit. I imitate my mom's mannerisms. "'Be sweet! Do good! Make me proud!'"

Kylie giggles and scoots closer, doing an impersonation of hers. "'Don't be hanging around any oddball folks.'"

"Oh my god. Mine too!"

"Better stay away from Wynn, then," Kylie says, teasing. I bristle at that, but Kylie keeps pushing. "Are you, like, good friends with her and Sully? I see you around them a lot. But they don't seem like your type of people. They're a little . . . *you know.*"

A flash of anger shoots through me, but I try to tell myself maybe Kylie doesn't mean anything by it. Maybe she's just parroting her mom. I think she's noticed her comment made me uncomfortable because she changes the subject.

Reaching over, Kylie gently combs her fingers through my hair, gazing into my eyes. "It's so pretty and long. Mind if I play with it?"

Too many feelings happen at once, and my brain's circuit breaker trips. I'm still mad at the things Kylie just said about my friends. I hate that she just called my hair "pretty." I'm melting over the way she's touching it. It's irritating that she likes how long it is when I despise that more than anything. I wish she liked me-me, not Mom's Maggie Grace version of me. I wish Sparrow from the dressing room could hold Kylie's hand, and that she'd want to hold mine back.

It's too much to process.

I open my mouth to say "I need to go" when the doorbell rings.

"Sparrow, dear!" Kylie's mom calls. "Your aunt is here!"

I rush downstairs, confused and relieved. But one look at Mags's face tells me I miscalculated, badly, coming to Kylie's house—I totally needed permission first. Lines of worry replace Mags's usual peaceful expression, and she leans into the doorway like she's checking to make sure I'm safe. For a second, her expression reminds me of Mom.

"Sparrow!" Mags cries when she sees me. "Thanks so

much for your hospitality, Lydia. We'll have to try and return the favor sometime."

Kylie's mom almost sneers. "Oh, that's not necessary. We stay very busy. Bye now!"

Mags is very quiet on the way home, and I can tell I've flubbed it, big time.

"I'm sorry," I mutter finally. "I thought it'd be okay."

Mags sighs and reaches over to give my knee a quick pat. "I can see how you'd think that—we haven't really talked about rules besides Wynn's house. I don't mind your going places with Wynn's and Sully's families because I know and trust them. And I may say yes to other folks, too, but let's have a plan first, okay? I need to agree to where and when, and I want to give you a cell phone, too, in case you run into trouble and need me to come get you."

I nod. That all seems reasonable. And I'm excited about having a phone. But it makes me feel worse for scaring Mags, especially considering the rude things Kylie said about Mags and everyone at Rainbow House.

When we get home and Mags goes inside, I sprint out to my orphaned garden plot, just in case November or Azul are still there waiting. They're not, and the plants don't look so great. A couple of tomato vines have completely collapsed into saggy, shriveled heaps from the intense heat. The sun is still grilling everything now at four o'clock and won't let up for hours.

I groan, panicking. I'm picturing all the plants collapsing one by one and myself getting a big giant zero on this project. Maybe if I water the plants hard now, they'll still stand a chance? I haul over the hose from the rainwater reservoir tank, then turn it on, chewing my bottom lip until it bleeds. Water trickles through the plot like a river, but it doesn't seem to want to soak in.

"Sparrow!" Wynn stands at the edge of the garden, calling across to me. I jog over, sheepish. Kylie's words still burn in my skull, and I hate that I heard them.

"Hey. Sorry I disappeared on the bus."

"Yeah, I was worried about you!"

"I went to Kylie's to help her with some homework."

"Oh." Wynn's face looks like she has things to *say*, but she doesn't.

"I don't think I'll go back over again, though," I admit. "Her mom's kind of rude." *And so is Kylie.*

"Fair enough," Wynn says, relaxing a little. Then, she toes the dirt. "So, question—how's your monologue writing coming along? Not to rush you! It's just, Sully and I have to work on our parts still, you know? Is there anything I can do to help?"

You can help me finish the last items on the List, I think. But I can't tell her about my deal with Shadow—that's probably a little too creepy, even for Wynn. "Maybe if we did something fun, it could help my mind work better?" I hint.

Wynn shrugs. "I'm game. What are you thinking?"

Hmm. Doing something just for giggles *and* something on the List sure would change my mood. "How about . . . a horror movie, and then you give me a haircut?"

"YES, PLEASE. I can finish my vocab homework while we watch. *Beetlejuice* and *Frankenweenie*—just let me find my good scissors!"

Watching old scary movies with Wynn is a balm for my soul, and for four solid hours, the worried noise in my head disappears. I can't help but notice the difference between how I felt at Kylie's house—almost like the Mom-version of myself—and how I am at Wynn's. Mr. Soderlund fixes us grilled cheese sandwiches, and I let myself sprawl out on the carpet like I do when I'm alone as I chomp down. I holler at the screen with Wynn, punch the air during the good parts, and act like a total ham.

It's getting close to bedtime when Wynn busts out the hair scissors. "How short are you thinking?"

"My mom's weirdly obsessed with my long hair," I say, twisting my mouth. "She'd probably hide the scissors if she was here. So, like, maybe not *too* much?" I motion to my shoulders: one *snip*.

"One mild-mannered haircut coming up!"

It doesn't take Wynn long—she's really good at cutting an even line. And, I'm not gonna lie; it feels good to see those seven inches fall onto the floor like a vanquished enemy.

I look in the mirror. It's not quite what I always dreamed of, but hopefully it's good enough for Shadow.

"Thanks, pal," I whisper. "I love it."

And I do. *Almost.*

Chapter Thirteen
Sparrow's Awful Feelings

Sparrow Malone

Mr. Fullilove

Science Essay, Seventh Grade

Sometimes, a flower evolves to mimic something
an insect is interested in, to attract it. For instance,
it might have petals and a scent that mimic a female
bee in order to trick male bees into acting as carriers
for its pollen.

Bee orchids did exactly that to attract a fuzzy little
solitary bee called the *Eucera longicornis*. (I like to
imagine them with little unicorn horns.) The orchids

and the bees went together like mustard and soft pretzels for thousands of years, until, sadly, the bee's population began to decline across Europe.

Now, the orchids are more common than the bees, and because plant adaptation happens slowly, the flowers still look and smell like the female Eucera longicornis, even in places where the bees don't exist anymore. And since the orchid is now able to self-pollinate, its old survival strategy probably seems a little weird to anyone who doesn't know about how it used to need the bees.

Mags and Luca haven't noticed my haircut—for some reason, I'm worried they'll react the way Mom would, so I keep my hoodie up until the next morning to hide it.

It's for nothing, though, because they're both outside the whole time I'm getting ready for school. On my way to meet Wynn at the bus stop, I see Mags and Teacher Rose talking by the rainwater tank. November is in the garden, too, tromping in rubber boots and rolling up the long water hose. The water hose I was using yesterday.

Whoops. I pull my hoodie strings tighter and walk fast, heart racing. *No, no, no! I got distracted and left the water on all night,* I realize. I glance over my shoulder to see the giant plastic water tank is completely empty. All the plots surrounding my adopted garden are covered in puddles, like after a week of heavy rain. Shadow tries to grab my hand and pull me back to the garden, pointing. I growl, panicking, and pull away.

It's obviously my fault—everyone knows. The hose leads right to my plot, naming me as the culprit. I can't tell from far away if anyone's face looks angry, but they must be, right? Not only did I flood several plots, but now, in the late August heat, the whole community's water tank is empty without a cloud in sight.

Wynn's chasing after me, but I'm hoping I can get on the bus and figure out what to do—how to apologize—before I have to see anyone's disappointed face.

"Sparrow, hold up!" Wynn shouts down the driveway.

I wish she'd lower her voice.

Wynn's all sweaty by the time she reaches me, her short faded green curls stuck to her face and neck. "Good grief, my legs are *short*, Sparrow. You go too fast." She frowns at my hoodie. "Aren't you hot in there?"

The bus pulls up just then, and we both climb on. I yank off my hood. "I messed up, Wynn," I groan. My hands tremble. "I left the hose on all night long, and everyone's gonna be so mad!"

"Yikes," Wynn says, wincing.

"Yeah." I clam up and can't say anything else all the way to school. Wynn offers to walk me to class, but I remember the commotion she caused trying to cheer me up yesterday, and the principal's and Kylie's scornful looks in the hall. I tell her I'm fine.

Kylie's not in math today, which is a relief. Focusing is hard enough—I'm worried about talking to Mom again this weekend, plus facing everyone from the garden when I get home. To top it all off, progress reports are due in drama today, and I have absolutely nothing to show for my monologue.

During science, Mr. Fullilove reminds us that report cards go out next Wednesday. He also squints and asks how my garden project is coming. He reassures me that even though my official grade will be low, not to worry because he'll boost it with my makeup credit later. I lie and say it's going great. I'm sure my chances with the orphaned plot are totally blown, but I'll think of something else before

Wednesday's report card. Even if Mr. Fullilove is understanding, my mom won't be, so something has to give.

I pass Wynn several times in the hallway, and she tries to flag me down. But ever since yesterday I can't stop seeing her through someone's, like Kylie's or Mom's, eyes. Wynn never plays it safe, and she doesn't mind being a walking, talking *scene*. As much as I'm drawn to her, right now, it feels like bad luck to stand out like that. I duck my head and keep walking. *I'll make it up to her later, away from school*, I think.

A bundle of nerves, I can't stomach lunch—so I decide to head to the library instead. I find a corner and pull out a notebook. Shadow squats in front of me, tilting its head this way and that. "Make yourself useful," I hiss, eyes stinging. "I've done most of the things on the List. That should buy me a little help, don't you think? If I don't turn in something to show progress today, it'll end up on my report card!"

Shadow is a fiery black opal today, and when it touches my knee, a jolt of electric energy zings me. "Cut it out!" I yelp. "*Fine*. Don't help. I'll make up a few paragraphs today and do the rest of the List this weekend. But then you gotta hold up your end of the deal."

Scowling, I start writing. I keep the monologue factual

and scientific. *Sparrow Malone's species is* Homo sapiens, *descended from countless human ancestors,* I write. *Sparrow learned how to read at the age of four, has eczema in the winter, and is red haired due to a mutated gene located on chromosome 16.* I scribble away at the monologue draft until my hand cramps and the bell rings. I dash to class, refusing to look at Shadow.

When I get to drama, Wynn and Sully wave me over. "Sorry I wasn't at lunch," I tell Sully. Then I stretch the truth a bit. "Had to put the finishing touches on this monologue."

"Last night's fun did the trick, then!" Wynn ventures, shooting a nervous glance at Sully, who looks relieved.

"That's awesome, Sparrow. We knew you'd come through," Sully says, fist-bumping me.

My ribs tighten, and I fake a smile. I turn in my rough start at the monologue to Mr. Fitz and settle onto the rug.

"Okay, team," Mr. Fitz calls. "Today, since we're exploring emotional identification this unit, I've asked our school counselor, Miss Young, to share about tapping into our feelings, and ways we can channel them. I'll be over at my desk, reading up on your monologues. Give her your respect and undivided attention!"

The word *counselor* sets my teeth on edge. Several

people, including Mags, asked if I'd be willing to speak to a counselor right after Mom went into the hospital. I'd said no, because what would be the point? They'd just ask questions I don't want to answer. *But Miss Young doesn't deserve attitude*, I remind myself. She's just here for drama class.

Miss Young smiles. Despite myself, I like her instantly. Her big hoop earrings sway as her gaze sweeps over the group in welcome. "I'd like us to start with a simple exercise. No one's gonna be put on the spot—don't worry. Let's all get comfortable"—she rests her dark brown hands just below her collarbone—"and place our hands on our heart, belly, or lap. We're gonna close our eyes, too, so nobody feels self-conscious."

I dutifully follow her instructions, trying to copy her calm expression. I can do peaceful. *I'll be so hard-core peaceful, maybe she'll notice, and mention it to Mr. Fitz*, I think.

"Feelings"—Miss Young's voice rings—"aren't out to get you, though it might feel like it. They can pop up out of nowhere, can't they? And sometimes, that might even feel a little embarrassing since we weren't expecting them to come on so strong. But while they can surprise us, if we check in with them more often, they help us understand ourselves."

My fingertips dig into my sternum.

"Right now, let's just notice how our bodies feel."

Like a ball of fire is in my throat, and my head is full of bees.

"Notice any tightness or places where you're hunkered over or clenching your muscles . . ."

My legs. My shoulders. My chest and belly.

"Take a minute to ask that part of your body, 'Hey, what's that sensation about?' If we wait for an answer, chances are, an emotion word might pop up. Words like *scared, resentful, disappointed,* or *excited.* Once you have your word, try saying, 'I feel this way because . . .'"

I obediently try. *Body, what is your deal? Why do you hurt all the time, stomach? Why do you hunch constantly, shoulders?* I'm asking because I'm supposed to. But I already know what the problem is; this exercise is making me uncomfortable.

Because the answer is simple. I have two kinds of feelings: the ones that keep me and Mom together, and the ones that don't. The first kind keep us safe, keep people out of our business, and keep me charging toward my goals. The rest, I club over the head and lock in the basement of my heart. I suspect if I ever let them out, they'd be *so* angry at me.

Why do people like Miss Young and Mr. Fitz act like feelings are so simple, and if you just express them, things will be fine? I have plenty of feelings that would never be fine, not even in 4.543 billion years (the approximate age of the earth). The way I feel about girls, for instance. Or how my nails dig into my palms when Mom lies. Or how scared I am that she won't get better—and that her troubles might get too big for me to carry. What then?

What about how I'd feel if she found out and didn't understand . . . *that I'm not a girl.*

Oh god. One of my hands flies up to cover my mouth, because I accidentally let myself think the words. And I know they're true. I am not a girl. And if Mom finds out . . . I think my entire world might change, inside and out.

I peek out of one blurry eye, and see Shadow peering into my face, inches from my nose. *This is all your fault,* I think. My feelings were neatly organized until Shadow showed up and started blurring the lines between my safe emotions and the terrifying ones. It's dangling the one thing I care about—Mom—in front of my face like a hostage, and I have to do everything that makes me wish, want, and ache in order to get her back.

I've been sitting here thinking for longer than I realize, because Miss Young has stopped talking. Everyone around me is stretching and gathering their things to go home. I wipe my cheeks before anyone sees they're wet. I shoulder my bag, but before I can bolt out to the bus, Mr. Fitz stops me.

"Hey, Sparrow, quick word about your monologue! Nice hair, by the way," he says, waving me to his desk.

"Thanks," I mumble, swallowing hard.

"So, I notice your writing is really technically . . . correct." His head bobs encouragingly. "But the assignment is about what makes you Sparrow on a more personal level. Like, for instance, what's your guiding light? What's your personal worldview—how you decide right and wrong? What makes your heart happy? I'm looking for answers to those sorts of questions."

I stare at him. My ears aren't doing their usual instructions-garbling trick, but they might as well be. Because it dawns on me: I don't . . . have a lock on *any* of this stuff. I have Mom, and deals with mysterious Shadows, plus heaps of stomach acid. It's a little humiliating.

Mr. Fitz softens. "Hey, listen, this is a challenging assignment! These are big questions, and lots of people your age are just starting to explore them. That's the point, right? So go explore!"

"Okay, Mr. Fitz. Thank you. I'll try."

"I have faith in you, kiddo. You'll get it."

I don't really have a choice, I think. So, I'll finish the deal with Shadow this weekend. Then the assignment will fall into place—it has to. After that, I'll scrape all these messy feelings back into a box, if I can.

But first, I have to go home and face my royal botch-up in the garden.

When I step off the bus, November's waiting for me. Wynn pecks my cheek and whispers, "Good luck, my pal. It's gonna be okay."

I don't feel okay. November has an eyebrow raised under their ball cap, but they're not yelling. Which shouldn't surprise me—I actually can't picture November yelling at anyone. But still.

"I left the water on," I blurt. My voice squeaks off at the end and my face crumples.

"Hey, whoa, buddy! Listen—these things happen, yeah? Everyone makes mistakes."

"None that stupid and epic," I say, wiping my nose on my sleeve because it's pouring as badly as . . . well, water from the forgotten garden hose.

"Oh, pal. You should hear about some of the mistakes I've made before. Well, no—you probably shouldn't, on second thought. Let's just say, leaving the garden hose on wasn't ideal? But it's also not the end of the world. It could be way worse." November unties the purple bandana from their neck and hands it to me.

I blow my nose, following them to my flooded garden plot. "Yeah? Like how?"

November blows noisy air from their cheeks and motions for me to follow them up the path. "Welp, when I was seventeen, I did a lot of things I shouldn't have. Including some bad choices that led to a drinking problem."

My jaw pops open. Partly because this is shocking, but also because November's talking about it so openly. It feels rude to not respond, so I ask: "What happened?"

"I went to rehab. I was lucky, too, because one of my friends was sent to the juvenile detention center instead. Not everybody gets the help they need, you know? The world can be really unfair. My grandpa's work buddies collected money to pay for my counseling. And after that, I kind of realized I wanted to do something good with the support they showed me."

It feels weird to hear November talk about themself like

this. Part of me is riled up, ready to defend their character. "But . . . but you weren't a bad person, though."

"Nah, I wasn't! But I was hurting from some stuff. And I didn't know how to help myself yet, so I tried solving my pain in ways that ended up hurting me more. After that, I had some tough patterns to ditch. And I couldn't break them alone. Nobody can."

I nod. I can't help but wonder if November knows about Mom, but I don't ask.

We near the garden plot, and I'm surprised to see it's not totally doomed—the tomato plants in particular are loaded down with fruit. But the vines are breaking off in places. November explains that the rest of the garden should be fine until Sunday, when it's supposed to rain. "Things'll perk back up, you'll see."

"So, today, we're adding stakes to these tomato vines. We'll drive bamboo pieces into the dirt beside the plants and anchor branches onto them with old nylons. That way, all the weight from those big, gorgeous fruits won't split these fragile vine joints that can't support them."

We work quietly, November humming a tune with the cicadas and soft cricket songs and me munching a tomato here and there, until the job is done. My arms are stronger from working in the garden, I notice. More covered in mosquito bites, too.

As I gingerly tie off the last vine, I think: *Maybe this is me and Mom. I'm too fragile to support her.* But I'll get stronger soon, and my super-student status will, too, with Shadow's help.

And as for all these gnarly feelings the List is bringing up for me, well, I buried them all before, didn't I? How hard can it be to stuff them back down again?

Chapter Fourteen
Sparrow, Snooping

Sparrow Malone

Miss Briscoe

ELA, Sixth Grade

The word *"simile"* means: a turn of phrase that compares one thing to an entirely different thing. Similes paint an interesting mental picture, like in the phrases "quick as lightning" or "fighting like cats and dogs." Sometimes, popular similes catch on like wildfire (get it??). But if the comparison is based on a myth, one of these catchy phrases can spread misinformation.

Take, for instance, the idea that someone is drawn to a bad habit "like a moth to a flame." Most scientists think moths aren't actually obsessed with fire. Instead, one theory suggests that nocturnal moths use the moon to help them orient themselves at night—distinguishing up from down—which helps them better navigate across the earth. Other theories state that moths use the moon's light to show them unobstructed escape routes through foliage when in danger.

When moths see fire, they probably think it's something helpful. But since it's too hot and way too close, the moths become confused—their species never evolved to reach the moon, much less circle it. So they dance round and round the searing flame or artificial light, thinking it's showing them the way. They might realize it's dangerous, but just as they break free from its orbit . . . they get fooled all over again. I think a better simile would be "Trapped, like a moth around a flame."

Early Saturday morning, I text silly photos to Wynn and Sully, to make up for avoiding them at school yesterday. Turns out, they're both busy—Sully's family is going hiking and Wynn's taking flowers to the cemetery with her dad. I'm a little relieved since I want to finish the rest of Shadow's List alone.

I wait around for Mom's phone call. When it finally comes, her voice is fragile and over-cheery—all brightly dyed Easter eggs in need of careful handling.

"Guess what, baby? I can have visitors Wednesday afternoon!"

A huge smile spreads across my face. "That's so awesome, Mom! I can't wait to hug you! I, um"—I pause, reaching up to my sort-of-short hair—"I have a surprise for you, I guess. I cut my hair a little bit."

There's a tense pause. Mom's words finally come out clipped. "Did my brother take you to the hairdresser? Just where does he get off, doing that without my permission!"

Mom's words feel like a slap, and my heart sinks. "Aunt Mags is a lady, Mama . . . you know that, right? And no, *she* didn't take me." I can't help it; I lean in on *she*, because it doesn't feel right hearing Mom disrespect Mags like that. It's unsettling to hear Mom disrespect anyone at all—usually she's too nervous to say boo to any other adult. The phone shakes a little in my hand. "My friend Wynn did my hair at her house."

"Who is this Wynn?" Mom demands. She's getting a familiar keyed-up edge to her voice—the one where she's tried to do good for a long time, and it's starting to wear on her. "I'd like to think I can still decide whose house you visit, Maggie Grace."

"They're real nice people, Mama, really." I need to calm her down before things go nuclear. "I've only been there and one other place—Kylie Funquist's house. You'd like them, I think, Mom."

"Is that Lydia Funquist's daughter?"

I blink. Sometimes, I forget Mom is *from* Brightbarrel, and she might know some people here. I hope Mom likes the Funquists, and that I didn't just add gasoline to her fire. "Yes?"

"Oh. Well. It's all right for you to go there, I guess. It's nice to know you're around some normal folks," Mom says, sounding calmer. "How are your grades, baby? Are you keeping your chin up?"

"I am," I answer quickly. "I'll have a report card to show you when I come there."

"That sounds so good, Maggie. And just make sure you dress up nice when you come, and let these people know how much you miss your mama. This whole thing really got blown out of proportion, and I believe it'd help if people saw we're okay. Maybe they'll let me leave sooner. I'm about ready to crawl out of my skin in this place."

What November said about pain yesterday—how it drives people to make bad choices—pops into my head. I know I'm supposed to bring up Mom's past today, to help finish off Shadow's List, and suddenly . . . November's words and Mom's past feel somehow connected. I grip the phone tight. The words are sticky, like they don't want to come out, but at last I ask:

"Mom? Do you think your shadows . . . your sadness . . . maybe caught up to you? And maybe you really do need help with it? You could talk more about what happened at Windy Hall. Might be nice if you didn't have to keep running." *It'd be even nicer if I could stop running with you, too*, I think.

Mom's voice is whispery, and I can tell her more honest—and more helpless—side has taken over. "I don't know about that, Maggie. I just don't know that it would help." She says it like a secret, and I know if I bring it up again later, she'll pretend this part of the conversation never happened.

"You could try, though, couldn't you?"

"We'll see, baby. Mostly I think we just need to keep moving."

My stomach tightens. "See you on Wednesday, Mom."

"I just don't know how much longer I can stay here."

"You can do it, Mom. See you on Wednesday," I insist, making my tone firm.

"All right, baby. I love you. Wear your nice shoes."

It's just me and Shadow for the rest of the afternoon.

Shadow looks especially strange today, prowling on all fours with its arms and legs elongating and shortening unnaturally as terrain demands as we navigate the property around Rainbow House. I'm following behind it, notebook in hand, reviewing the List.

"If we finish this dumb thing today, you can spend tomorrow helping me with the reflection monologue," I direct quietly. *But after that, then what?* I wonder. Will Shadow disappear when I leave Rainbow House to go back to Mom? Or will I be stuck with a strange, gangly cosmic-looking demon hallucination until I outgrow my boots?

And what about me?

Shadow waves me on with a "follow me" gesture. Muttering, I stalk after it until we're standing on the front steps of Rainbow House. *Windy Hall.* I swallow and shake my head.

Shadow crawls up the steps, craning its head to see through the windows. My brain starts playing a game called: Guess What Shadow Is Thinking. Right now, it's probably thinking: *Aren't you curious, Sparrow?* A violent shudder travels across my back.

You've always wanted the truth about the whole universe, Sparrow. Why not this corner of it?

I shift, uneasy. "To help Mom, right?" I ask aloud.

Shadow shrugs, which I imagine means: *Sure. If it helps you to see it that way.*

I gaze up at the old house. Laughter drifts from one of the college students' apartments upstairs—maybe November and Azul's. I can hear someone listening to music through the open window in the kitchen, plus plates and silverware clanging. Can I just go in? It is my aunt's house, technically, but other people live here and this seems like intruding.

But I follow Shadow inside anyway, dashing past doorways to avoid being seen. Somewhere in the house, an occupant burns something like smoky lavender. A shower hisses upstairs. Shadow glides down hallways and up two staircases until finally we stop in front of a little door. I jiggle the handle. It's locked. Shadow slips through the crack beneath the door and disappears like a whisper. I wait. *What now?* Slowly, the lock on the handle rotates, then the handle twists until the door creaks open. It's dark on the other side, and all I can see of Shadow are its glowing orb eyes, winking.

Its eyes widen a bit as if to inquire, *Well? Shall we?*

I won't feel fear. I square my shoulders and lift my jaw, imagining I'm a knight braving a cursed tower in order to save my mother. I fumble my hand around for a light switch. I find one, and sputtering yellow light fills the closet. Right in front of my face is a ladder leading up to an attic. The attic where Mom got sent to hang out with the bats.

November boarded it up, so they can't get in anymore, I remind myself. Besides, I've seen the little brown bats. They're cute.

Shadow climbs up ahead of me. Hand over hand, I follow it up the ladder and into the dusty gloom. It's . . . an ordinary attic. Musty, but neat. There are lots of boxes with different names on them—probably Rainbow House residents using the attic for storage. One reads "Azul" and several more are November's. There's even one with Aunt Mags's old name—she calls it her deadname. I understand this, because that's exactly how "Magnolia Grace" feels to me—*dead*. It feels bad to even read it.

Some of the boxes are open. "Snooping" is on my list, but going through their things doesn't sit right with my gut.

Shadow hovers in a far corner beside a grimy window, pointing at something. I walk slowly, not wanting the boards to creak. Shadow struggles to dig its fingers into a crack on the boards of the attic floor.

Wordlessly, I thrust my fingers into the cracks alongside Shadow's, prying the board upward. To my shock, it lifts easily. I'm surprised Shadow couldn't move it alone.

Something lies beneath the floorboard, nestled atop yellowing foam insulation. A plaid shirt, maybe? I lift it, and it's heavier than I expect. Unwrapping the cloth, I discover a little journal with old cartoon cats on the cover. I open it and find my mom's name in tiny, perfect letters: *Abigail Malone*.

Looking at it would be just as snoopy as peeking in boxes. But somehow, it feels less wrong to poke around in Mom's secrets. They run my whole life, after all. It only seems fair that I should know *why* I spend so much time putting us back together, over and over.

I flip to the first page and begin to read.

My mouth falls open as my eyes race across the delicate, threaded handwriting. My tongue goes bone-dry after a while, making me wish for water. The light through the attic window fades, so I tuck the journal under my arm and wander home in a daze, then disappear into my room in Mags's trailer, fall on the bed, and weep.

I can't even think properly.

There's one last item on my list: country music, and right now it feels like the only thing I can imagine calming the storm that's roiling around inside me. I use my phone to find a sweet-but-lonesome song by a new country singer, Emmett Maguire. I listen to it over and over until I know all its yearning words by heart. After that, I memorize songs by John Prine, Rhiannon Giddens, and Dolly Parton while I lie on the floor and stare out my window at a hazy waning moon. Tears puddle in my ears. Something about the way the fiddle sings and how the steel guitar cries helps ease the sting in my heart.

The rest of the evening, I stay in my room with my boots

on, because being with people hurts too much, but so does being alone. Shadow perches at the end of my bed, never leaving, watching me as I comb through Mom's journal over and over.

What I'm reading doesn't make sense. It could never make any sense to me, and my world is spinning. Finally, exhausted, I kick off my boots and crash into dreamless sleep.

Chapter Fifteen
Sparrow Taking Shortcuts

Abby Malone

Journal, age fifteen

Dear Diary,

Can't write long today b/c my hands are covered
in blisters. Mama & Daddy found the note I wrote
to Amy—I didn't even send it and I wasn't going to.
I just needed to get my thoughts out. Is it wrong
to love who I love? Daddy says it is, so I spent all
weekend digging holes, then filling them back up

again. I dug twenty, until finally Mama saw my hands and cried and told him I'd learned my lesson.

I don't know what I'll say about my hands at school. But Daddy says, "Better to have bandaged hands than a filthy heart." Does calling Amy my sweetheart make me bad, though? Daddy and Mama think so. Mama keeps trying to set me up with pushy Gabe, but I can't think of him that way. He's too old and kind of a creep. Guess I'll play along with it, though, if it keeps me from digging more holes.

Sully and Wynn both text me on Sunday, but I'm not in the mood. My eyes are still swollen from last night—so bad that Mags offers me some allergy medication.

I pick at my breakfast, then hurry to strap on my boots. The List is complete, and I half expect Shadow to disappear like a traitor now that its source of kicks and giggles is exhausted.

But as soon as I put them on, Shadow unfurls.

I'm glad to see you, Shadow seems to say.

"Yeah, well. Time to pay up. You ran my heart over with a lawn mower, and it's never going to be the same again, so now you really have to help me. Monologue time."

Shadow holds up a single finger. *One more thing.*

"That's cheating, you insufferable nether-thing!"

Shadow shakes the raised finger a single time, insisting.

It's not like I have a choice. I cross my arms tight across my body and huff as I follow it into the living room. It hovers in front of the rolltop desk. The desk where Mags put those official-looking papers from Mom's hospital stay.

"No way. Mags is right there in the kitchen," I hiss. "And anyway, I've snooped enough, wouldn't you say? Now my life is ruined."

Shadow cocks its head as if to say *How?*

I won't answer that. I storm outside instead, nudging Bela Pugosi out of the way and slamming the door, but Shadow follows me. I ignore it and tramp out to my adopted garden plot, hoping I'll calm down while I take pictures for my science project. *If I can turn it in tomorrow,* I think, *my report card will look amazing on Wednesday when I go see Mom.* But when I try to envision Mom's face lighting up, feeling proud and coming out of her funk, the victory feels hollow.

It's not enough anymore. Pulling Mom out of her tail-spin doesn't make me feel like a hero, I realize, because part of me is *angry* with her. And I feel so guilty about that.

"You knew what I'd see in that diary," I growl, spinning toward Shadow and jutting my chin. "You knew, and you let me find it anyway. So what do I do? I still have to help Mom, and now I don't even want to look at her."

Shadow stares.

"Because Mom *knows*. She knows! She lived with so many rules that were so unfair, just like me! And she knows exactly what it feels like. At least partly. Mom liked girls, Shadow! And she's mean about it anyway. What am I supposed to do with that?" I claw my fingers into my hair.

Memories of Mom insisting we dress and act in people-pleasing ways loop in my mind. When I was little, I'd even had nightmares about giant eyeballs staring into our apartment windows, scrutinizing my every move. Every parenting choice Mom made was an effort to impress folks—I'd always known that. She hadn't really cared about organic spinach or school dress codes or crushes on boys. It was all for show. I'd assumed all she wanted was to draw attention away from her own sadness and addiction. But what if she was scared for me, too?

Maybe Mom thinks if she can hide my queerness, she can protect me from hateful people like her and Mags's parents. Maybe Mom sees that part of herself as dangerous.

I wrestle with that for a minute. It's twisted, but if you lived a life like Mom's, it would make sense. A deep ache fills my chest as I realize: Mom's all alone. She always has been. There are so many people who have accepted me since I came to Rainbow House. And who did Mom ever have as a kid? No one, once Mags left home.

My true north—my urge to protect Mom—tries to flicker back to life.

"Maybe things can change. If Mom knows it's okay to be herself . . . maybe she'll accept me, too. But I think people need to be with folks who care about them, Shadow, before they can get better. So will you help me save her?"

Shadow jabs a long finger again in the direction of the trailer.

We're back to fighting over the rolltop desk.

I growl, tipped well past the limit of my temper. My brain goes white. I claw at the laces of my boots, undoing them and hurling them away from me in a fit of cussing and tears, not caring where they land. Shadow vanishes. Good. Forget Shadow. Forget the deal. I'll save Mom myself. I can't believe I've let myself become this sidetracked. It's time to knuckle down. I scrub my bleary eyes and stand, readying to take photos of the garden for my project.

And then I see that I've thrown my boots right into the biggest, nicest-looking tomato vine, which is now broken in several places and dangling pathetically in pieces from its stakes. "Crud," I mutter, heart racing. Everything else in the plot is okay, but not nearly as impressive as that ruined bush of Brandywine tomatoes.

I pace in a couple of slow circles, holding my belly. *Think, Sparrow.*

Okay. Desperate times, desperate measures. My stomach churns as I form my plan, because it's not pretty. But I'm seeing Mom on Wednesday and it feels like I have no choice. I need to turn in something spectacular before then, so Mr. Fullilove will add the makeup credit to my report card grade.

I skulk around the garden until I find a showstopping plot. In the education section where Sully's parents teach, there's a native pollinator bed full of flowering herbs, russet-colored sunflowers, bee balm, cone flowers, and black-eyed Susans. In wobbly cursive, someone has labeled each plant on smooth stone markers.

My stomach hurts. *Don't overthink it*, I tell myself.

I snap the photos from several angles. Bees are a keystone species—a topic Mr. Fullilove adores talking about—so I'll be sure to include that it's a Tennessee native plants pollinator garden in my project report. I can say this is my adopted plot instead of the tiny one I just wrecked, which will win me "good person" points, too.

Which is ironic, because right now, I feel anything but good. I feel horrible, and I'm glad Shadow isn't around to blink at me. But what else can I do?

My rib bones squeeze so hard, I picture them curling in and stabbing me in the heart. I feel ashamed and worlds away from the Sparrow I saw in the dressing room mirror last weekend. But even more than that . . . I feel scared. Scared of losing Mom. What if I can't save her?

I sprint for the community garden toolshed, where the volunteer sign-in list sits inside on a wooden shelf. I scan until I find Azul's and November's signatures, and snap a photo of those, too.

The rest of Sunday, I use Mags's printer and a posterboard to create a collage of photos and attach my project report to the back. After an hour's practice, I forge my mentors' signatures at the bottom, confirming I put in my work hours. My heart is hammering out accusations at me the whole time, but at this point, what's another injury to my feelings?

If it's for Mom, it's worth it, right?

Chapter Sixteen
Sparrow Breaks Everything

Sparrow Malone

Mrs. Garcia

ELA Homework, Purple

Natural Communication

When comparing a honey mushroom and an aspen, you might not think they have much in common. One is a fungus, the other a tree. But both species hold the record for being the biggest known living organisms on our planet, depending on how you measure them. That's because both species have enormous root systems.

A single mushroom network in Oregon, connected by underground fibers called mycelia, covers over three square miles of forest. And a single grove of aspen trees near Salt Lake City, Utah, contains forty thousand individual tree clones, all united by the same root network. Both of these organisms can send nutrients and hormones between individuals. When something happens to one, they're all affected.

I'm too late for the bus Monday morning, so Luca drives me to school. Even though flip-flops are technically off-limits at Brightbarrel Middle, I wear them anyway—I don't want to see Shadow again. Luca attempts chitchat, but I'm so nervous about the day ahead, I just respond in grunts and nods.

My science poster is rolled tight under my arm as I check in at the office and head to my first class. In the foyer, I see the gym teacher talking to Wynn. He frowns at the holes in her jeans and her snug-fitting shirt. "That's not code, Miss Soderlund."

"My shirt is the same amount of tight as three people who have walked by just now, including that guy!" Wynn insists, pointing. *She's right*, I think. The boy nervously scurrying past has a shirt that fits basically the same.

The gym teacher looks flustered, and mad about it. "That's different."

"Why? Because I'm *chubby*? Because I'm chesty?" Wynn shouts. A curious crowd gathers, and a couple of teachers stick their heads out of doorways to see if everyone's okay. "That's not fair at all. I'm every bit as clothed as him." Wynn spots me, and her eyes flood with relief. "Sparrow, back me up!"

The gym teacher's gaze shifts to me, and one eyebrow slides up. Everyone's watching. *Please don't notice my flip-flops. Please don't think I'm a troublemaker.* My pits are a total swamp, and the urge to shape-shift—to blend in completely—kicks in. I clutch my rolled-up poster, duck my head, and keep walking like I've never met Wynn before.

All the way down the hall, I can feel Wynn's stare burning a hole in my back.

That's my first disaster choice of the day.

My second comes after a morning of taking a stressful math test, realizing I forgot my ELA homework this weekend, dodging Wynn in the hallway, and marching to science with my imposter project in hand.

Mr. Fullilove's mustache twitches this way and that as he surveys my poster and scans my project report. "Well, Sparrow, I'll admit I was concerned when you handed this in so early. One week is less work than I'd like to see for such a big part of your grade. But if you promise to keep it up for the next three weeks and have your mentors sign off on it, I'll apply it to your report card on Wednesday."

I'm so relieved, I could cry. "Thank you so much." I go to return to my seat, and he calls, "Um, just a moment, Sparrow . . ."

My shoulders lock. I turn slowly, ready to hear I've been found out.

"This is an excellent example of attention to detail and initiative. May I hang it up on the classroom wall?"

Guilt pummels me, but I smile weakly, nodding. "Sure thing, sir."

Disaster number three strikes right after lunch. I'm hustling into drama, double-checking for my faithful essay collection in my bag, and gearing up to give Mr. Fitz my practiced speech about how unfair his expectations are. I decide to approach him after class, since that's when he last ambushed me.

I move to sit between Wynn and Sully like usual, but they both look royally hacked off. My first thought is: *Maybe they're beefing with each other?* But then I remember how I bailed on Wynn in the foyer this morning and realize it's probably me she's mad at. I've never seen her like this, arms crossed and nostrils flared, and I'm not sure how to handle it.

Whenever Mom's mad, she wants me to joke and loosen her up. I decide to give it a shot with Wynn. I stick my pencil between my upper lip and my nose, holding it there like a mustache, and waggle my eyebrows at her.

Wynn's anger is full of unmovable conviction, though, and looking into her intense face is like staring right into the sun. She's not having my clowning. Her eyes sweep the ceiling before looking away. Sully's quiet beside her, picking at the carpet. *Probably as uncomfortable as I am*, I think.

Mr. Fitz tells us that today, we're to break off into our groups and work on our monologue collaborations. I swallow hard, knowing I need to clear the air with Wynn before we can get to work. Then, I can tell them I still don't have the monologue written and beg for patience. In the back of my mind, I'm already concocting a plan to ask Mr. Fitz if

Sully or Wynn can be the subject of the monologue, and I'll just write it up nicely.

"Sooo," says Sully, staring at the ceiling. His hands are jammed into his fuzzy peach cardigan and his mouth is tense.

That's my cue. I take the plunge. "Wynn, I owe you an apology. I'm sorry if you feel like I ditched you today. I was having a bad morning. Forgive me?"

Wynn's eyes flare and crackle. "I forgive you, Sparrow. But you should know that's a terrible apology. You've been a bad friend lately. Yeah, because you *acted like you didn't know me* this morning. But also because you've been avoiding me in the hallway, too, and not just today. I can tell when someone doesn't want to be seen with me, and it really sucks."

My heart's pumping at warp speed. Everything Wynn says . . . is true. And I don't have a single excuse. I guess I'd hoped she just wouldn't notice. People from other groups are turning to listen, and my face scorches.

"Okay," I say. Then I clamp my mouth tight, because I have no idea what comes next. What am I supposed to do?

Wynn excuses herself to the bathroom, and I swallow hard. Sully sketches something next to me quietly.

"Sorry about that scene," I mumble.

"You're sorry Wynn has feelings?" Sully asks, sucking his teeth.

"Um, no, I mean . . ."

"Mind if I ask you something? I saw your poster in science. It looked good. But why'd you do it?"

I frown, confused. "I . . . when I moved here, because . . . my mom got sick and my grades got messed up. Mr. Fullilove let me do some extra credit to fix them."

"Oh, no, see—that part, I get. I'm in Fullilove's class, too. I'm actually doing the same project because my grades on the first couple of homework assignments were in the toilet."

"Oh."

"Yeah, so, imagine how surprised I was when I walked in today and saw *my pollinator project* up on the wall with your name on it." *Oh no.* My stomach drops all the way to my shoes and my neck's flaming.

Sully finally looks at me, and unlike Wynn's fiery eyes, his are flat. Terrifyingly flat, like he's gone behind a wall, and I'll never see him again.

"Sully, I—" I stop, because what do I say? Tell him about

Mom? Yes, I decide, I'll do exactly that, because I can feel my friend slipping away from me faster than my mouth can move. "My mom's in rehab," I blurt. "She's not sick, she's in rehab, and I really needed the grade to help her feel better."

Something I can't name flashes across Sully's face, but he's still not budging. "I'm sorry about your mom, Sparrow. I wish you'd told me sooner. But you should know I'm dyslexic. And even though I go hard and I'm smart, school still takes extra work sometimes. My parents and I are always careful to find ways for me to honor my learning. My garden was part of that plan, Sparrow, and now I can't take credit for it." Sully drums his hands on his knees and shakes his head.

"I didn't know it was yours," I croak.

"Yeah, but you knew it was someone's. And you didn't even think about that someone getting hurt."

I need Sully and Wynn to forgive me, so we can move on to nailing the drama assignment. It's a selfish way to think about it, but I can't stop feeling desperate. "Sorry," I say. "I'll find a way to make it up to you! Can we talk about the drama assignment now, please?"

"I don't know, Sparrow, I need a minute."

The rest of the period passes awkwardly, and we get a whole lot of nothing done.

At the end of class, Wynn still isn't back, and Sully rolls his eyes a little as he leaves. But I can't get sidetracked. I'll think about all that later. Right now, I have to confront Mr. Fitz.

I wrestle my folder from my backpack, march over to Mr. Fitz—shaking from adrenaline—and slam my old essays onto his desk harder than I mean to. He manages not to look surprised and instead folds his hands calmly. "Hey there, Sparrow. How can I help you?"

I launch right in. "I'm not a philosopher or a poet or a feely-feely person, Mr. Fitz. But I'm a good writer. These essays prove it. Every last one of them is an A, from the past five grades. I'm asking your permission to interview someone else from my group and let me write about their identity instead." I raise my chin.

Mr. Fitz studies me for a long minute, then nods. "Okay, Sparrow. I'll tell you what. I will agree to read these grade A essays and consider what you've said—"

"Seriously? Thank you, Mr. Fitz!"

"—if you promise to ask a friend to help you, and if you

give the monologue one more honest shot from your own perspective."

My triumph caves. Shadow won't help me unless I snoop in Mags's desk. And my only two real friends just walked out the door, refusing to talk to me. I bite my lip, then nod. "Okay. Deal." But I have no idea how I'm going to pull it off.

Chapter Seventeen

Sparrow Puzzling
It Out

Abby Malone

Journal, age fourteen

If I have a daughter someday, I'll never force her
to eat anything she doesn't like. I will never push her to
like mean, "upstanding" boys she's not interested in.
She'll never have to sleep in the attic, I'll never take
away her mirrors, and we'll watch movies together
and eat ice cream every weekend. I'll tell her she's
pretty and paint her bedroom pink for her and never
say her long hair is "starting to look like something

the cat dragged in." I don't want to get married, but if I do, my daughter will always know she's the sweetest girl in the world.

Tuesday in math, Kylie pokes me in the shoulder with the eraser end of her pencil. "You look like the library just burned down or something," she whispers. "What gives?"

I haven't talked to Kylie much since that day at her house when she was dunking on Wynn and Sully. And I still don't want to, exactly—I already feel bad for the way I let them both down. But when Kylie reaches over and softly runs her fingernails across my back, I melt inside because it feels really nice to be touched. Teacher Jones has stepped into the hallway for something, so I whisper back, "I'm stressed over a couple of classes." It's not a lie.

"My mom and I are having a 'treat yourself' day after school. We're going to get our nails done, grab burgers, go to the salon . . . Come with us."

I hesitate. Mags isn't wild about Mrs. Funquist, and I really should try to fix these things with Sully and Wynn. Plus, November and Azul still expect me in the garden after school—though I'm not sure how I'll look them in the eye after forging their names.

But the soft way Kylie's gazing at me feels so nice. It makes me feel likable again, and, pathetic as it is, I could use some of that, even if it's coming from sharp-tongued Kylie. Besides, it's not like anyone else will hang out with me.

"Okay," I say. "I'll call my aunt in the bathroom at lunch."

On the phone, Mags isn't thrilled about me spending more time with Kylie, I can tell.

"Last time you went over there, you looked kinda tense, kiddo. You sure about that idea?"

"My mom says it's fine," I say, feeling defensive—of myself or Mom, I'm not sure—even though Mags is right. "She likes that I'm spending time with the Funquists."

Mags sighs on the other end of the line. "All right, hon. I love you, do you know that? You are a *good kid*, Sparrow, just the way you are. And I'm proud of you. If you need anything or to be picked up, you have my number and Luca's."

I choke on my guilt. Mags wouldn't be proud if she knew everything I've done lately. Mom wouldn't, either, for that matter, though there's just a skinny Venn diagram overlap between "Things Mags Likes" and "Stuff Mom Approves Of." I suspect I've managed to fail by both their standards.

"I love you, too, Aunt Mags. I'll call if I need to."

I don't go to drama after gym. Instead, I hide in a bathroom stall until school's over. When I meet Kylie in the pickup line and we slide into the Funquists' SUV, part of me is giddy to escape everything that's been on my mind—the garden, the thing with Wynn and Sully, my nerves over seeing Mom again on Wednesday . . .

That happy bubble pops quickly, though, as Mrs. Funquist starts in on Kylie.

"Where's your new jacket that goes with that outfit? Did you not wear it this morning?" she says, frowning and examining Kylie in the rearview like she's a specimen in a petri dish.

Kylie's arms stiffen. "Mom, we have *company*," she says meaningfully.

"Sparrow doesn't seem to mind," Mrs. Funquist snaps without pausing to check if that's true. "Now, when we go into the nail place, you tell them you want a nice, cute color that doesn't draw attention away from your hair."

"Mom," Kylie groans.

In the restaurant, Mrs. Funquist chooses Kylie's food, declaring her daughter "should really just have a salad." I have money left over from what Mags gave me, so I smile sweetly and order for myself: an enormous grilled cheese and a milkshake with two straws. Every time Kylie's mom opens her mouth, I think of my harsh grandparents in my own mother's diary. I insist on sharing my food with Kylie, slyly playing dumb while using my best manners.

Beneath the table, I feel Kylie's fingers thread into mine. "Thank you. I like you, you know," she whispers into my ear while her mom's in the bathroom. I cock my head, trying to tell if she means *like* as a friend, or *like* as in . . .

Our booth is around the corner from the main dining area, and no one else can see us. Kylie leans in and closes her eyes, brushing her lips against mine for a split second.

Oh. Yes, she likes me like *that*. I'm trying to process how this escalated to kissing? And I kind of wish she'd do it again, because I'm dizzy in a nice way.

Kylie's complicated, I think. Because she's clearly queer, like me. Maybe she's like Mom, and she's prickly about things because she's afraid of being judged herself. But what if we could be there for each other? That would be a relief. Suddenly, I want to tell her who I really am—nonbinary. Because it feels important to me that she knows. But before I can pluck up the nerve, Kylie's mom is back, and it's time to go.

We go into the beauty salon, and Mrs. Funquist checks

Kylie in for her appointment. I sit in the waiting area, paging through beauty magazines. Some of the haircuts are really outdated—so outdated they're almost back in style again. Mrs. Funquist is talking loudly over Kylie's protests, explaining the exact color and cut Mrs. Funquist wants for Kylie's hair, and soon the stylist gives Kylie an apologetic look and sets to work.

Kylie shrinks in the chair. A fire lights in my belly, watching them. Maybe Kylie's mom is doing what she thinks is best, but she's running right over Kylie like she's not even there. And while I can't help noticing the similarity to my own life, somehow it's easier to feel riled up on Kylie's behalf.

A goateed young stylist in a smock arrives behind the cash register. "Do you have an appointment?" they ask. Their hair is every hue of the ocean, meticulously curled.

"Oh, no. I'm just waiting on my friend to be done with her torture session," I quip, unable to hide my saltiness. Mrs. Funquist is still pestering Kylie's poor hairstylist, managing to insult Kylie's body in several different ways as she nitpicks.

"Nice cut you found there," the stylist says, pointing to the magazine in my lap. I glance up at the lapel of their smock, and I see a nonbinary flag pinned there, like the one on November's hat. I grin.

"Thanks. I've always loved short hair."

"I'm an apprentice here. I have a slot free now. Want a cut?"

My fingers move up to snip, snip. *Yes, please*, my soul asks.

Mom would flip, I remind myself. But part of me—the new, confident part that's afraid of disappearing again— wants something permanent that can't be given away once I go back to living with Mom. Plus? I don't like Mrs. Funquist, and my gremlin temper wants to prove that she can't control *everyone*.

"I only have a ten."

The young stylist smiles broadly. "Works for me. C'mon."

I follow them to an open chair, and they ask if I want the pixie style in the book.

"Kind of," I say. I motion for them to lean closer, and I whisper instructions.

"Oh yeah! That's gonna be awesome."

Twenty minutes. That's how long it takes for me to achieve my lifelong dream. My red hair is cut in a short fade up the sides and falls wavy at the top. I stare at my reflection. The person looking back at me is new but also so familiar. Cute. Handsome. Just right. I feel like 330,000 pounds—the entire weight of an adult blue whale—has been lifted off my body.

Hello, you, I think, swiping my eyes with my knuckles. I pay the stylist, then impulsively hug them. I feel like I'm floating up into the sky, giddy and powerful. I can't stop touching my short hair, a little thrill filling my heart each time my fingers brush the fuzz. I grin like a fool all the way out of the salon.

In Kylie's SUV, she texts me.

Your hair is *different*, girl.

The AC feels so cool on my neck and ears, and I feel an electric zing of joy every time I catch my reflection in the car window. I'm feeling so bold and right, I decide it's now or never. I text back:

Can I tell you something?
I'm not a girl. I'm nonbinary.
Maybe leaning a little to the boy side.

Kylie doesn't respond. Instead, her face flushes fuchsia, and she glances at her mom in the driver's seat. Mrs.

Funquist's elegant face looks strained in the rearview mirror. Her black-rimmed eyes keep cutting sharply from the road to my hair, then narrowing. I hear a noise like someone sucking their teeth as her glossy fingernails tap out an execution drum rhythm on the leather steering wheel. Then, as if she's decided something final, her lips clench as she shoots Kylie *a look* over her shoulder.

Kylie goes pale. She turns toward her window the rest of the way to Rainbow House. Several times, I reach over and poke Kylie's leg, hoping to get her attention. But Kylie might as well be a cement statue. If I didn't know better, I'd guess she's fallen asleep—but she's turning her cell phone over and over in her hand like a worry stone, and her shoulders are hunched and tense.

Maybe I shouldn't have told Kylie about being nonbinary, I think. I wish I could snatch the words back, and my stomach is a sour pit of dread. *Why did I tell her?*

Right before we pull up in front of the turnoff, Kylie texts:

Y I K E S.

Sorry Sparrow.

But honestly? That "not a girl" stuff is so weird.
I wouldn't tell that to anyone else if I were you.

I'm stunned. Maybe Kylie doesn't understand what non-binary means. Surely if she knew how huge this is—how important it is to me—she'd be more accepting. I climb out, then pop my head back in the car. "Can I call you later?" I blurt out. "Maybe I can explain better." I reach over and try to take her hand the way she took mine at lunch.

Kylie yanks her arm away like I'm a snake trying to bite her. "Honestly? I don't think we should hang out again. Bye, Sparrow." The car drives away with the door ajar.

My entire body storms with feelings I don't know how to weather at once. I kick off my flip-flops and start jogging down the long driveway. Movement is such a relief, I break into a full run, not stopping until I hit Mags's trailer door.

By the time I'm in the kitchen, I'm crying so hard I have the hiccups. Mags materializes in nothing flat, and without asking any questions, she wraps her soft arms around me.

Finally, I'm calm enough to drink some water, and we sit down at the table. I can tell Mags notices my hair, but she's waiting for me to explain.

The whole story tumbles out: my worry about Mom, how I took credit for Sully's garden project, the way I didn't stick up for Wynn . . .

But when I get to Kylie, I slow. I want to say a few important words by themselves, apart from the hurtful Kylie story. It feels right to give them their own space.

"Aunt Mags, I like girls. Or maybe just . . . anyone, whether they're a girl, a guy or, like, something else." *Like me.*

Aunt Mags smiles and pats my hand. "That's a wonderful thing to know about yourself," she says. "Thank you for trusting me with it."

"And—" I close my eyes and take a big breath. Right now, it feels important to not pretend—to not be hiding at all behind "Maggie Grace." I want to be every bit Sparrow when I say this. I squeeze my eyes shut and speak from my gut. "I'm not a girl. I'm more like a boy but not quite. I'm nonbinary, Aunt Mags."

When I open my eyes, my heart lifts to see Mags smiling softly and nodding. "I'm so glad to know that about you, Sparrow. I see you. What words would you like me to use for you?"

I want to say *they* and *them*, because they're mine. But I also want a little time to use them myself first. And I'm not ready for Mom to hear them. Mom may never be ready. *How will I ever go back to my old life now?* What's even the point of trying out perfect words I'll never get to use? But more and more, hearing *she* disorients my heart and feels like an uncomfortable shirt that doesn't fit right. "I think . . . maybe you could just use my name for now."

"Shall I tell Luca to do the same, just at home?"

"Yeah, I'd like that." I start crying all over again because telling my aunt and having her understand—it's a huge relief.

I explain about Kylie, how she kissed me, how her mom bullied her, and how Kylie unceremoniously dropped our friendship when I came out to her. Mags's lips purse several times, and her eyebrows try to launch off her face at the end, but she doesn't interrupt or say "I told you so." She just pats my back, hums in empathy. "That must've really hurt. I'm so sorry.

"I wonder if we can talk again about how worried you are over school," Mags adds after I blow my nose. "It seems like that one assignment has you really frustrated."

"It's a reflection monologue about 'what it means to be me,'" I say sourly. "And it's impossible. I sit down to write it, and—" My chest gets tight. I feel terrible inside. I have the urge to run. "I can't do it."

Mags sips some sweet tea. "Would you like ideas, or just need someone to listen?"

"Ideas! Please," I say with a barking laugh. I'd choose anything over more painful deals with Shadow.

"I have a friend who says everyone's born with three magic cauldrons inside them. One is for survival, and when we're born, it's upright, ready to receive love. The second is self—it begins sideways, and only experiencing genuine emotions in your own shoes can turn it. Joy, sorrow, grief, adventure, risk . . . That's where our creativity comes from."

I nod. The metaphor makes sense. I feel most alive—most like myself—in moments when I don't have to playact as a perfect student or as Maggie Grace. Like when I watched the bats that night, felt my muscles burn from garden work, or got swept away by the beauty of the blackberry thickets. Even back when I did my secret walk under the covered walkway at my old school, I felt it.

"You said three cauldrons, though. What's the last one?"

"That one turns for master storytellers, sages, and extremely old folks." Mags laughs. "And it turns by getting really, really good at the second cauldron." Mags pats my hand and gets up to stretch. "Anyway, just a thought. Maybe you know yourself better than you realize."

I go to the bathroom, then see my phone has a new message. It's from Kylie.

Sorry about before.
My mom was listening.
Listen I have a crush on u and we can still
b together at school if you act normal.

I lean against the bathroom counter and fire back:

what do you mean 'normal'?

I mean just don't be extra.
U don't need to be a boy or whatever.
Just act like a normal girl.

I wipe sweat off my palms, scowling and breathing deep. Kylie's text hurts, but I notice I'm not panicking. I even stop myself from firing back my first snarky knee-jerk response. I can smell perfume on my shirt from the monster hug Mags just gave me while I was crying. Somehow, remembering how chill and supportive my aunt was gives me steel. Knowing she has my back makes me feel like *somebody*.

That gives me space to sort my thoughts: I feel bad for Kylie. Seriously, her mom's yellow-jacket mean. But I also can't make myself smaller—less than Sparrow—just for Kylie, even if she flips my heart like a pancake. *I bet my difference scares Kylie because her mom is so critical of her*, I realize. So, she pushed me away to stay safe.

Exactly like I did with Wynn, I think. *Ouch.* I get now why my lousy apology wasn't nearly good enough, and remorse grips my heart.

I think for several long minutes, then know what I need to say to Kylie.

> I don't love how that feels, Kylie.
> I am who I am, and I deserve better.
> And so do you.

Exhausted, I power down my phone. I take a shower, washing the little hairs from the salon off my neck. Then, I ask Mags if I can stay home tomorrow, because I'm having cramps and my brain feels wrung out like a sponge from the past several days. I don't have any big assignments to turn in—except my one last try at the essay. And I need to think long and hard about what I want to say to my friends before I face them again.

If they'll even listen to me.

Also . . . tomorrow, I see Mom again.

I stare up at the shadows on the ceiling. Drinking down deep breaths, I cradle two worlds in my head, side by side. One, I've created here at Rainbow House with a new, just-right self that bursts with constant feeling—pain, longing, joy, embarrassment, courage, cockiness, daring. It's like I've popped my eyes open in the world, finally awake.

And the other world? It's with Mom. But the balance of that life is fragile, and I'm exhausted from trying to keep it from wobbling and crashing. It's so familiar, the idea of losing it flips a switch inside me that renders me as feral as any caged badger (North American, not European). I would do—scratch that—I *have done* everything in my power, even things I'm ashamed of, in order not to lose it. I've even disappeared myself.

I should be psyching myself up to see Mom tomorrow, going over the finer points of how to cheer her up, be what she needs, and get us back on track.

But now that I know saying yes to Mom's world means saying no to my new one?

I don't know what I want anymore.

Chapter Eighteen
Sparrow Unraveling

Sparrow Malone

Mr. Fullilove

Science Essay, Seventh Grade

Unfinished Report

Once, a scientist wondered what might happen to a bay in northwest Washington when he removed all the purple sea stars from a designated area. (The sea stars are apex predators, meaning they are at the top of the food chain in their ecosystem.) Since they eat so many other organisms, he wanted to see if their absence would help the other sea creatures in the bay flourish.

So the silly scientist hurled all the purple sea stars into deeper waters. I'm sure he meant well—he hypothesized the remaining animals would thrive after the bruise-colored stars had been banished. But just the opposite happened. One by one, the limpets, algae, barnacles, sea slugs, anemones, and chitons just vanished. It turns out, the sea stars were necessary all along for life to maintain its balance—

Wednesday morning, I still can't decide how I want to look when I visit Mom. I could borrow a hat from Mags, but it's not like Mom won't notice. And while I could wear my comfort outfit—Mom's used to my shorts, sweatshirt, and flip-flops—she asked me to dress nice on the phone. But all my old clothes are too small, and anyway, I break out in sweat whenever I think about putting them on again.

I just can't.

So I go into the bathroom and do my new hair, adoring

the look and feel of it. I put on my shirt with the little dinosaurs and my perfect jeans, which I roll up at the bottom, so they won't get wet as I wade out into the dewy garden to retrieve my discarded boots.

They lay right where I hurled them, tangled in the broken, wilted tomato plant. Beside the mess, there's a rock with a ridiculous sad face painted on it. A speech bubble made of pebbles reads, *Come back, Sparrow!* I smile to myself, sheepish. *Azul, I bet.* I rearrange the pebbles to say, *Sorry. Okay.*

I lift my boots gingerly and shake the spiders out of them. Grimacing, I swipe at the little trails of dried snail slime tracked across the leather. "Sorry, boots," I whisper. Then I squat for a minute and stare at them, my toes digging into the soft dirt, trying to figure out what to do until this evening.

I know I decided to stay home and rest, but I can't sleep. I could still see if Mags would take me to school. Even though I can print my report card from online, I know I should face Mr. Fullilove and tell him the truth about Sully's project. But the thought of doing that and seeing Mom in the same day churns my belly. *One thing at a time*, I decide.

I could do what I promised Mr. Fitz, though, and give my monologue one last shot. Even though I still want to impress Mom with a stellar presentation, my need to conquer this is about more than just a grade now. I've never met an assignment that I've failed so spectacularly at. It's become personal, and I'm intrigued. *Why is such a silly thing mopping the floor with me?*

But to finish it, I need Shadow's help.

Or maybe I don't? Mags's words from last night replay in my head. *"Maybe you know yourself better than you realize."* If experiences—living in your own true life—are what help you know yourself, I guess it's true I've had a ton lately.

Thanks to the List.

My lips part and my brows scoot together. "Wait, shut up!" I mouth-breathe as I pick up my boots and study them. "Shadow, if you're in there, and I know you are, you little life-ruining twerp . . . I'm considering the possibility that maybe you aren't an evil chaos demon that feeds on rebellious acts. Which makes you *what*, exactly?"

Is it possible Shadow was trying to help me? What if it wasn't making a deal. Maybe I never needed a deal at all. Maybe Shadow understood the inner-cauldron-turning assignment long before I did, and was trying to help.

But it wants me to look in Mags's rolltop desk, I remind myself. Every time I think about doing it, I get a sick feeling in the pit of my stomach. Maybe because I'm afraid of what I'll find, and worse, I'm afraid I won't be able to handle whatever it is on my own.

But I'm not alone, I remind myself. I have people. And Shadow.

My feet remember their way into the boots, and Shadow is there, bending the sunlight like a prism. *Love the hair,* Shadow seems to say.

"Rolltop desk," I answer.

Mags and Luca are out. So I follow Shadow into the trailer, knees shaking. My fingers slide beneath the crack under the desktop, but it's locked. I run and grab a screwdriver from the junk drawer in the kitchen. Shakily, I jam it into the lock, fiddle with it until something clicks, and gently lift the lid. It takes a moment of shuffling to find the pages with my mom's name on them, but then there it is: *Abigail Malone.*

The words are stark in black-and-white. It's so jarring to see a whole person—my well-meaning, sometimes panicky, always beautiful-to-me mother—boiled down to her very worst mistakes. My eyes skid across them all, unblinking. She stole medication from the elderly man in her care. She took three times the recommended dose. She passed out while driving and ran our car over a fence and into a family's yard. The family wasn't home, thank goodness. Paramedics saved Mom's life with medicine that reversed her overdose. Worst of all, Mom can't take care of me again unless she keeps getting the help she needs—court order. My mom . . . is really in trouble.

"Oh, Mom," I moan softly, sinking onto the floor. I feel like someone's punched me directly in the gut. Seeing the facts written out like this, in a way I can't soften, makes me realize I'm in way over my head. "I can't fix this."

But I knew that already, I realize.

"Because of the diary," I say aloud to Shadow, scrubbing my eyes. "Mom's problems are complicated. For the record? I would have rather Mom shared that stuff with me herself."

I curl up on the floor, paper in hand. Bela Pugosi licks the tears off my face, and Shadow rests a comforting hand on my foot. "But she probably wouldn't have," I admit. "Mom needs so much help. And I do, too."

"Sparrow?" The front door creaks, and footsteps thump across the carpet. Mags's voice is alarmed, then resigned. "Sparrow? Oh dear. Honey, come here." I'm a snotty mess in Mags's arms again—I'm starting to make a habit of it—then after a while, Luca presses a warm mug into my hand.

"Cioccolata calda, extra chocolate, extra marshmallows," Luca says.

I sip for a minute, leaning against Mags as we both sit on the floor. Mags wipes her eyes with her thumbs and lets out a long sigh, but she doesn't look angry.

"Just so you know, kiddo, any time you have questions about your mom, you can ask me. And I'll do my best to be as honest as I can. You don't have to poke around alone."

I nod. Mags's voice is so gentle, once again offering me a safe place to land. This time, I let myself fall into her arms, hiccupping with out-of-control sobs. The disappointment in my heart hurts as it rushes out, but it's a relief, too, to finally let go of the weight. Mags smooths my hair and makes comforting shushing noises that sound like wind in dry grass.

"Why didn't she get help before?" I whisper finally. "If she was having such a hard time, and she knew we could end up like this—why won't she admit she has a problem?"

"Maybe she thought she could protect you from the truth and spare you the hurt, love. People can sometimes do very wrong things for the right reasons," Mags murmurs.

True, I think. That's something I can relate to a lot lately.

Mags asks if I want to watch a movie on the couch, and I nod, curling up under a granny square blanket and dozing off as *Ponyo* plays in the background. Mags doesn't say anything when I don't take off my boots, and I'm grateful. I'm not ready for Shadow to leave again.

When I wake again, it's almost dark. Mom always said that's how I reset after a spill on my bike or an argument: I power down and reboot like a computer. Warm air laden with bonfire smoke drifts in through the screen door, and something savory is cooking in the kitchen.

Wait. It's getting late. *My meeting with Mom!* My aunt's muffled voice comes from the patio outside, and Shadow and I scramble off the couch and out the door to remind her we need to go, Bela yipping excitedly at my heels. "Mags? Aunt Mags, it's almost eight!"

Mags is on her cell phone, her face tense. I clamp my mouth shut and jam my hands in my pockets, waiting impatiently.

"I see. No, I understand. Please let us know if—all right. Thank you so much, ma'am." Mags lets out a long, ragged breath and pats the patio chair beside hers.

I sit, nibbling away at the inside of my cheek. "What's wrong? We can't go? We're too late?"

"Sparrow, I'm so sorry, but your mom left the recovery center early. She checked herself out, but we don't know where she is."

Chapter Nineteen
Sparrow Coming Home

Sparrow Malone

Miss Thibodeaux

Science Homework, Fourth Grade

Did you know that even if you cut a tree down all the way to the ground, sometimes it grows back? The tree can replicate its cells until it sprouts a brand-new trunk. This is because half of the tree is hidden away from sight. Beneath the earth's surface, in the darkness and quiet, there are roots that stretch as deep and wide as the branches themselves. This is how it saves itself.

*

As soon as Mags tells me Mom's checked out early, pain slams my chest and tears flood my throat. I read the papers. I understand what this means. For me to live with Mom again, she has to do what the court says. Leaving early means she's giving that up. "Why? Why would she do that?"

"Oh, darlin'. I'm so sorry," Mags says softly. "She may still try again, yet. Healing is difficult."

Panic rises. "What's going to happen to me?"

"Sparrow Malone—listen to me. I am your family. So is Luca. That won't change, no matter what. You always have a place here."

But I can't listen. Because it's all too complicated, and my body needs to *run*. "I'm going out into the garden," I blurt, then take off into the dusk.

I fly past the bat boxes streaming with little brown bats. I run double time to the song of the cicadas—two footfalls to every drone cycle. I sprint past a wall of perfumed honey-suckles until I'm at the blackberry thickets, where someone's rustling in the vines.

November emerges, carrying a bucket and slapping mosquitoes. Their face furrows when they notice me. I guess

I look pretty snotty. "Hey, buddy, feel like talking?"

"My mom left rehab early," I choke. "And now I can't live with her."

"Oh. I'm so sorry. That's heavy."

"It just feels really, really bad to know that if someone has to choose between you and the thing that's bad for them . . ." I trail off, because even though I'm thinking it, it feels too horrible to say out loud.

"Oh, pal. Maybe I can help there? Not to excuse your mom! But to help you not hurt yourself with thoughts like that? May I?"

I don't want to keep up this crummy Malone tradition of refusing help, so I nod. "Sure. Shoot."

"People can be in so much emotional pain—from stuff that happened long ago—that their bodies get off-kilter, and they look for relief in the wrong places. It's not that they like what they're doing. It's that they need help from skilled folks. *Grown* folks. Does that make sense? You literally couldn't be awesome enough to magic someone's pain away."

"Yeah?"

"Yeah. When I was having trouble, my grandpa was awesome. My brother was amazing. But it took a whole big community of people being really patient for a long time, and a lot of tricky emotional work, for me to get better. Not everybody gets that chance. But your mom's lucky—a lot of cool people are supporting her if she's able to let them. It may take a while."

I'm hugging my knees, sitting on the grass. As November talks, somehow, underneath all my disappointment, I feel a growing relief. I don't have to fix it. I couldn't even fix it if I tried.

"Also? It's okay to be mad, Sparrow. Whatever you're feeling, it's okay to feel it. Feelings just *are*."

"Thanks, November."

"You bet, pal. And you have people around to talk with whenever, too, okay? You don't have to be so tough."

I nod. "I think I just need to think for a while."

"Totally understandable." November pats my shoulder and pads away, whistling softly. I sit and stare at the blackberries. The flowers look pink in the rosy light. For a long bit, I gaze at them, letting my heart slow. I've been tensing myself against all these feelings for so long, trying to white-knuckle Mom and me into success. But now Mom's given up, so what's the point of resisting them anymore? I'm so tired. I let my eyelids fall and put my hands on my chest like the school counselor showed us, feeling a little corny. And I let the flood wash over me.

I feel . . . Crushed. Uncertain. Angry. Enraged, even. Betrayed. Hurt.

I'm feeling this way because . . .

Mom gave up. She let me work my behind off and make everything about her for so long, and then, *pfffft!* See ya, Sparrow. Which leaves me not knowing what to do next, because not only did I lose her, I also lost parts of myself along the way. She's yanked my world out from under me so hard, I'm seeing stars.

Mom and I have been doing this dance together since I was small. I always knew just how to cheer her up, snap her out of it, make her smile. It was exhausting, but at least I always had a way to feel important to her. She needed me to hold her together, and being needed felt nice. I made it my whole life. But now Mom's decided to go somewhere I can't follow. So where does that leave me?

Suppose November's right. Maybe . . . Mom's pain was never mine to fix. Maybe protecting it was the only way she knew how to connect—the only way she could let herself see me—so I latched on to the role of Abigail's daughter for dear life.

But now that we're not all tangled up, doing the same dance over and over, I could be anything I wanted, couldn't I?

I'm not the same Sparrow I was a few weeks ago—so much has changed. I don't know what comes next. I can feel a green bud of hope forming in my heart. I'm starting to imagine a life where it might be okay to be myself, with or without Mom.

And there's something I really want to do.

I dash back toward the trailer and slip in silently. Notebook and a pen are all I need. I race back out toward the bonfire pit beside the pavilion. No one's there—the Rainbow House residents have gone in for the night. But at the middle of the fire, a few embers still glow hot. Carefully, I lay the List atop the oscillating coals and watch an orange ribbon of fire transform Mom's Thou Shalt Nots into curling gray ash. I don't need it anymore.

I turn from the pile and walk away.

"Where are you, Shadow?" I whisper. Cricket song and warm air blow softly around my ears. "I just want to say thanks."

Across the garden, fireflies dance. With miraculous bioluminescence, they keep calling and answering, over and over until they find one another. A group forms like a little cloud of stars, then slowly they begin to walk toward me.

"Thank you for finding me," I whisper. "And for helping me find myself."

Shadow is made of glowing lights tonight. Cute. Handsome. Beautiful. Neither, both, and something else entirely. *And good and brave and kind*, I think.

Thank you for trusting me, and for not giving up. I was afraid we'd lost each other. That's what I imagine Shadow is thinking. Or maybe I *know* that's what Shadow's thinking . . . because the words are running through my mind, too.

"Losing each other is a garbage idea. Let's never do that again," I try to joke, chin wobbling. My heart is all fireworks and confetti as, slowly, fireflies land all over me in response, tickling my skin.

"I think I understand who you are, you know. Who *we* are. We're not Magnolia Grace. We don't have to pretend for anyone. We're not alone, either. You and me are 'we' and 'us,' together. We're just Sparrow, and that's okay. Not a girl. Not a boy. Just us. They and them!"

One by one, the lightning bugs flare, then vanish on my skin, filling my heart with a warm, spinning sensation. "I'm here," I say, tears streaming. I look up into the blue-velvet sky, and finally feel like I'm taking my place under the stars.

Chapter Twenty
Sparrow Tries Again

Sparrow's notebook

Textbooks teach how animals' defense mechanisms are crucial to the species' survival, but I notice not many focus on how the animals calm down again. Surviving attacks is important, but what if the creature didn't go back to normal life afterward? If a turtle stayed in its shell, it would starve. A deer can't run forever. Hognose snakes don't spend all their time pretending to be dead—otherwise what would be the point of living?

Knowing when to let your guard down and

live must be part of survival, too. Maybe that's as important a part of animal evolution as venom or horns or hiding.

Thursday morning, I feel fragile. Not like a brittle heirloom teapot everyone's scared will break. Fragile as in brand-new—like a blackberry shoot pushing up through a crack in concrete, or a brand-new swallowtail breaking free of its chrysalis.

I stayed up all night, writing a new list. This time, it's an actual bucket list that's all mine. I stash it in my pocket and glance in the mirror, grinning, before I dash out the door.

My hair? Absolutely killing it.

I think Shadow's in my thoughts still, but I can't tell the difference between us anymore—probably because there isn't any. I just have a deep, quiet *knowing* in my gut. It's small for now, but it's there. As Mags drives me to school and I walk through the hallway, I still have the urge to shape-shift, to get yanked around by people's expectations, to please. But that shadow-core of knowing? It keeps me walking in my own shoes.

In math, Kylie's at a new desk. I feel a twinge of sadness, but

I'm not surprised. And really—I get it. Sometimes, it's unsafe to take up space as yourself when you don't have enough support. Kylie's not a bad person. Just scared. It's a feeling I know all too well. *I hope things get better for you, Kylie*, I think.

When I head to Mr. Fullilove's class, my heart is in my throat. *It's time to come clean.* I've never purposefully sabotaged myself with a teacher before, but I'm not doing this for me—I'm doing it because Sully is brilliant, and he deserves credit for his work.

Mr. Fullilove looks mildly baffled as my words tumble out at top speed. I explain how my original transcript was wrong, but I didn't want to make trouble. And I confess that I took credit for Sully's garden plot. Meekly, I give him a new poster with photos of my real plot—not nearly as breathtaking as Sully's, but it's mine. November and Azul signed off on it this morning, for real this time, and accepted my apology by turning me into a November-and-Azul-hug-sandwich.

"Well, Miss Malone—"

"No Miss, please. Just Sparrow."

"Well, Sparrow, I appreciate your candor and willingness to do the right thing. However, considering the stress you no doubt caused Sullivan, and the considerably lower quality of gardening . . . I'm sorry to say this project deserves a C."

My ego is writhing in pain, but I'll survive it.

"Also, I'll look into your transcript and see if we can straighten out your overall grade. If you did the work in your old classroom, you should receive the credit. I'm glad you said something."

Next is lunch. I'm not hungry at all, but I go through the motions of getting food anyway and meekly walk to Sully's table. "May I sit here?"

Sully stares at me. He still has his guard up, and I can't say that I blame him. I've been a lousy friend.

"I was a complete dill weed to you, and there's no excuse for it."

Sully purses his lips. "Yes. You were. And?"

"And you've been nothing but generous to me. I was new and you were welcoming. You shared your stuff, supported me when we went shopping, and were there for me. I admire you so much, and I wish I were as confident and observant as you. You deserved the opposite of what I did."

"Hmm." Sully leans back in his chair, watching me.

"And I broke your trust. So, I told Mr. Fullilove that the project was yours. And I turned in my own dinky project, complete with a photo of a mostly dead tomato plant. I asked that he correct the name on yours, and put my new one up on the wall, too—that part's for you. I strongly suggest you go look at them side by side, because honestly, it's so embarrassing for me, it's kind of funny."

Sully's eyes flicker, but he's holding his poker face.

"Anyway, I understand if you don't want to be friends. But if I can make amends—do your chores, buy you makeup with my allowance, weed your garden . . ."

"Keep your death-kiss fingers off my flowers, Sparrow Malone," Sully says. "But fine. You have a second chance. Don't blow it."

I'm terrified to talk to Wynn, but I'm doing it anyway. I shuffle into drama at the end of the day, and we break off into groups to work on our projects. I take a deep breath and ask if I can sit beside her.

Wynn's eyes shoot daggers. "Are you sure you want to be seen with me?"

"I'm sorry I avoided you, Wynn. And it doesn't matter why I did it, so I won't try to defend myself." I chew my lip.

"I'd kinda like to know why, actually."

I draw another huge breath. "I was acting ugly because

I was scared. And I couldn't figure out how to honor our friendship *and* feel safe in my life. It makes me feel awful every time I think about it because you're amazing. I wanna learn how to be the kind of friend you deserve."

Wynn's eyes soften in acknowledgment, then blaze. "Wait, you didn't feel *safe*? What happened? Who do we need to fight?"

I grin at Wynn sheepishly and swallow hard. I want to start telling my friends more, because I realize I can't do everything alone. But this first time I'm trying, it feels as natural as walking through the good Walmart in your underwear.

"So, it's my mom . . ."

For the rest of the period, I tell her and Sully about Mom and how I'm staying with Mags for the foreseeable future. Sharing is still new and awkward for me, so I don't talk much about my feelings yet, just the facts. Baby steps. But I do tell them I'm nonbinary, and that I wished I could come out to Mom but I'm afraid to. Wynn hugs me until I think my teeth will eject, and Sully asks, "So, what are your pronouns, then?"

Am I ready for this? I check in with my gut. *Yeah, this feels okay.* "They and them. Thanks."

"Wynn, have you asked Sparrow when they're finally gonna write their part of our assignment?" Sully makes a show of asking.

I giggle. Even as my face is roasting with embarrassment over the unfinished monologue, I'm floating in outer space because I'm so gosh darn happy.

Wynn taps her chin and waggles her eyebrows. "No, Sully, I haven't asked them. But maybe they'd like to share their progress with us now?"

"I'm trying! It's been hard. But I think . . . I think I'm close, and I'm gonna ask Mr. Fitz for an extension."

The bell rings, and I approach Mr. Fitz and explain my situation. He agrees to give us an extra week so Sully and Wynn have plenty of time to work on costume, mini-set, and rehearsal. Before I go, he calls after me. "Sparrow, just a sec!" He pulls my essay collection from his desk. "You were right. These essays are honestly beautiful. You have a thoughtful and curious way of viewing the world, and your love of nature is obvious. Since you're most comfortable with that topic, I have an idea. What if you found a way to relate what you admire in the natural world to your own life somehow? You could use that topic as a bridge. And then take little steps across it."

That's true, I realize. If I stay in my wheelhouse just a little, it might be easier to branch out into unfamiliar territory. "I like that," I say. "I'll give it a shot."

Chapter Twenty-One

Sparrow Shining Bright

Sparrow's notebook

Why do we say things like "Let's get out in nature" or "We must protect Mother Earth"? When you think about it, we're as much a part of nature as any other creatures, aren't we? We're expressions of the universe, just like spiderwebs and nebulas and pecan trees and honeycombs. We're social mammals, we're omnivores, we have predator and prey instincts.

Humans just have complex brains, too, so we complicate life more than other animals do— especially our relationships.

We push each other away out of fear, and our loneliness hurts us. But if we try too hard to save each other, that hurts, too.

I think maybe we're not really heroes or little gods. We're just creatures. That's a big enough miracle all by itself, if you think about it.

By the time our drama presentation finally rolls around, Wynn, Sully, and I have been working during every free moment, making sure each word, sequin, prop, and gesture are just so.

After much lobbying and coordinating, we have special permission from Mr. Fitz to perform our monologue tonight in the learning pavilion at Rainbow House. This way, Wynn's dad, Sully's family, and Mags and Luca—along with my garden mentors and several more people I've befriended from the community garden—can watch us perform, too.

Secretly, I consider it my thank-you letter to them all, for being there for me.

I haven't heard a word from Mom since she left the recovery center. But I send her cell phone a text, too, inviting her to come to the performance. The likelihood of her setting a toe into Windy Hall is next to zero, but it feels good to know I tried.

Two hours before showtime, I'm happy to lend my muscles to help Sully transform our improvised pavilion stage into a fairy-tale garden full of flowers. I hang twinkle lights and suspend azure and swallowtail butterflies made from delicate paper—"a little to the left, now to the right!"—until finally Sully nods, smiling. It really is breathtaking. He's gonna be famous someday, I tell him, and he laughs.

Then I listen as Wynn practices my monologue one last time. A grateful knot gathers in my throat because she's made it a point to understand the exact feelings behind the words and conveys them flawlessly. Wynn's acting has this way of tugging your heartstrings skillfully, like a talented harp player, and when she finishes, I tackle her with a hug.

Right at the golden hour, when the sun starts to set and gilds the entire garden with magic light, everyone starts up the pavilion ramp and settles in the folding chairs we set out. I'm crouched behind a thin white screen, ready to dash out onto the lawn and switch on the bright back light as planned. Sully is poised to the side, waiting to start the background synth music and pull the props to the side on cue.

Mr. Fitz welcomes everyone and invites us to begin. The synth music starts, and Wynn holds a papier-mâché mask in front of her face and begins to speak, posing in front of a panel of fun-house mirrors.

"There are many shape-shifters in nature. They use deception, camouflage, mimicry to survive a difficult world. The anglerfish, the octopus, the bee orchid, the cuttlefish . . .

"And me." I can't see Wynn from behind the screen, but I know this part by heart: She drops the mask and does a spin.

"My strategy was this: to become what others expected, so I never surprised or threatened them. I learned to be comforting to everyone but myself, until I forgot my original form. I wandered through habitat after habitat, changing and morphing to stay alive, but never resting.

"Until I landed in a garden, where the soil was rich and warm."

Sully hauls the rope connected to the mirror panel, and it slides away to reveal his magical garden set. Appreciative ahhhs go up from our audience, and my heart skips with pleasure. Racing to the light, I flick it on, then take my place behind our homemade sheer stage scrim. My silhouette is bold against the fabric, creating a shadow behind Wynn that copies her as she moves.

"My shifting slowed, and for brief moments, I saw glimpses of my heart and the things it wanted. I saw it in bats and fireflies, who love the space between day and night. I noticed myself in sharp-smelling tomato vines that flourished on their supports. I related to the trees, who love creating protective shelter. I saw my face in blackberry thickets—being born, becoming, entwining, and growing old."

As Wynn recites these words, I dance and somersault and cartwheel, motioning for her to follow, just like Shadow did for me.

"But what do you say to yourself after you've been strangers for so long? How do you reclaim your form? And how do you avoid feeling silly, thinking no one might recognize you? That everyone might laugh? Some people might hate you, even. I sway between curiosity and hiding, curiosity and hiding."

Behind Wynn, I spin, starting with my arms open wide and slowly drawing them to my chest.

"I'm learning to be gentle with myself. I reach inside

my soul's DNA for blueprints without copying answers from anyone else's page. I melt. I rest. I wait. I become strong. I am light and darkness. I am neither, both, and something else entirely."

I stretch out my arms and pull the release strings Sully built into my sleeves. In a fluid motion, fabric unfurls from them to form shimmering butterfly wings. The crowd isn't supposed to applaud yet, but several people wolf whistle and cheer anyway.

"Little by little, I transform!" Wynn shouts in triumph.

Our little audience erupts into cheers, a bunch of beautiful, unruly hooligans clapping and stamping their feet until the pavilion floor vibrates. I emerge sweaty from behind the scrim, smiling shyly, then join Wynn and Sully for a team bow. Sully's big sisters are proudly taking photos on their phones and grinning. Wynn's dad blows a kiss, and her grammy is there waving around a shockingly large jar of pickles. I hear Luca shout "Forza, Sparrow!" and November and Azul are honking their noses into handkerchiefs.

Then, in the back row, I see Aunt Mags beaming as she gives a single jazz hand. Her other hand . . . is around my mom's shoulders.

"Mom!" I haven't stopped feeling hurt or angry, but I volley over props and around chairs to hug her anyway because . . . well, she's my mom.

She looks out of place and uncomfortable, but—right now, at least—there's no spacey fog in her expression. Mom's here, clear-eyed and alert. I don't hesitate. I hug her hard.

Immediately, she's a weepy mess. Part of me wants to think it's because she heard my monologue and understood what it meant, because wouldn't it be nice if Mom saw me? Like, *really saw me.* But her face is still shifty and distrustful of everyone around us, and I can tell it's taking much effort for her to stand close to Mags and stay polite. As everyone filters out of the pavilion and over to the bonfire pit, Mags excuses herself to the ramp and waits.

"I'm glad you came, Mom."

"You did real good, Maggie—"

"Mom"—I interrupt—"my name is *Sparrow.* I know we joke, but that name hurts me every time you say it." My heart is beating at the speed of light, but I know this is my moment. "I'd like you to call me Sparrow. And I need you to know . . . that I'm not a girl. I'm nonbinary. I'm non-binary and I'm queer, and I always have been. But I think you know that already. I think you've always known."

"Oh. Baby. We don't need to get into this now." She reaches up and touches my hair, then pulls her hand back to cover her mouth. *This is so tough for her*, I think. But the shadow in my heart reminds me that Mom's feelings are hers, and mine are mine. I don't siphon away her pain. Hers being real doesn't mean that mine stop mattering.

"I need to do this right now. Because I have some things I need to say. You have a problem, Mom. I wish you'd gotten help sooner. I'm sad because I had to be perfect, all the time, so that you could keep running from the truth, and I never want to help you hide again. I'll still love you. I just can't keep holding you up anymore. I have to have some room to be me, and I need you to see me."

Mom's face pinches. "That's a little dramatic. I know who you are!"

"You know who you want me to be," I say slowly. My face and neck are getting so warm, and my hands have gone sweaty and shaky. But I finish this while Mags and Luca are nearby—while I'm feeling safe and brave enough. "Just like your parents tried to make you be who they wanted."

I inhale slowly, trying to focus on how the floor feels under my feet. *I can do this.* "I found your journal."

Mom does a confused laugh, eyes darting around. "Oh, honey, I'm not even sure what you're talking about anymore . . ."

"The one upstairs under the floorboards, in the attic of Rainbow House—*Windy Hall.*"

Mom's face goes white, and her expression looks like she's just been electrocuted. Suddenly, I don't know what to say next. From my internet reading, I know that "outing" someone—telling other people that the person's gay—is always wrong, no matter what your reason for it. I don't want to do that. Should I let her know that *I know* she liked girls? Does it count as outing if I'm outing Mom to herself? I don't think so, technically, but . . . somehow, it still feels wrong. People should get to talk about things in their own time, even if they've hurt you. And I want to be gentler to Mom than she's been to me. I want to be cool about it, for my own sake.

"I'm sorry I didn't respect your privacy. I know your parents . . . weren't good to you. They didn't love you like they should have. They didn't leave room for you. But you and I could be different, Mom. Can we be different, please?"

Mom stands wordless for a moment, looking stricken. Thoughts wrestle in her sunken eyes for what feels like forever, and I start to fidget, feeling weird and awkward. I've broken all our unspoken rules . . . so now what?

Finally, Mom surprises me with a frantic nod. She can't meet my eyes, though. Her too-skinny hand trembles and hovers by my head a second like it wants to brush over my short hair again. Words struggle out around tears, her voice braided with strangled croaks and squeaks. "I know, baby. Seeing you on that stage, I just . . . I do want us both to be happy. I can't do it by myself. I don't know how. I'm so sorry . . . *Sparrow*." My name comes out with effort, but there's no denying it crossed Mom's lips. "I need your help."

My heart floods with grief. I *hate* seeing my mom look so broken and small, like a lost little kid. But if things are ever really going to change for us, I know I have to draw a line. "If you want help, you gotta ask people your own age, and let them help you. I'm just a kid, Mom." My voice cracks on the sharp edge of that truth, and twelve years of relieved tears drip off my wobbling chin. *I'm small. I'm the kid.* "And it's not fair."

I still want to confront her over her diary, and the hypocrisy of passing her pain on to me. Or point out how blending in never did her much good, anyhow. I could pry open dozens of cans of worms, because I know it might help her learn—

But . . . my gut tells me it's not smart for the two of us to get all tangled together again. Not right now. Mom has to find her own way.

She moves to hug me, but that's too overwhelming right now. So instead, I wipe my face and grab my elbow awkwardly, turning away. Mags strides over, then, drawing a ragged breath. "It's all right, Sparrow, I've got this," she whispers, squeezing my hand. I breathe a sigh of relief, nodding. A weight lifts off my shoulders.

"Abigail, I love you so, so much," Mags croons gently. Mom melts and collapses into her sister's shoulder, sobbing, and Mags wraps Mom up tight in her sturdy arms.

"If you decide to try again, there's always a place for you here," Mags is whispering as I inch away. "We can make a different life than the one we were handed, Abby. We can heal together."

I keep walking as Mom whispers something that's too far away for me to hear now. I decide that even though I'm so happy Mom showed up, I'm not ready yet to be around her when she's weepy like this. It's too easy for me to jump right back into playing her hero, and . . .

I need some growing space of my own.

Instead of turning back, I gaze out across Rainbow House's jumble-tumble garden. Cool evening air tickles my bare neck, and I feel my heart rate slowing, calming. Fireflies blink here and there, and the light in my heart answers back.

Yes. I'm here.

Wynn and Sully wave at me from the bonfire. Azul rides on November's back and laughs as they both spin in the yard. Teacher Rose is showing the little kids how to roast potatoes in the fire.

I wrap my glittery wings around my body. Sauntering away from the pavilion and across the yard, I let the sunset's riot of hues wash over me, bathing me in warmth and light. Somewhere, a mockingbird sings every song it knows, back-to-back. Cicadas thrum, mosquitoes whine, and I add my voice to the chorus, letting a happy hum buzz through my chest.

"Come dance with us!" Wynn calls as Sully spins her.

"Save me a spot!" I call, breaking into a run.

Racing toward the glowing bonfire circle, my strides match the rhythm of my heart. I adore the sound of my pulse in my ears—wild and vulnerable, tender and fierce.

I, Sparrow Malone, am no one's daughter. I'm no one's son. That doesn't make me nothing, though. Not even close. I am loved, so deeply, by so many, for everything that I am.

I am neither. Both. Something else. Being alive is something beautiful.

Resources for Readers

In the beginning of this book, Sparrow has a tough time due to a lack of support while facing several challenging issues. Sometimes, life can get lonely and scary. But Sparrow didn't have to go on alone, and neither do you! If you need extra support yourself or have a loved one who's experiencing a substance use disorder, here's a short list of help available to you.

Gender Spectrum is a national organization committed to the health and well-being of gender-diverse children and teens. This is a good place to find information about the language and issues often tied to gender diversity, stories from trans/nonbinary young people, and moderated online chat groups for pre-teens and teens. https://www.genderspectrum. org/articles/youth-faqs

The Trevor Project is the world's largest suicide prevention and crisis intervention organization for lesbian, gay, bisexual, transgender, nonbinary, queer, and questioning young people. Their counseling staff is trained to offer support 24/7. If you are in crisis, suicidal, considering self-harm, or just need an accepting place to talk to someone, call now at 1-866-488-7386 or text "START" to 678-678.

Substance Abuse and Mental Health Services Administration (SAMHSA) has a 24/7 phone service called the National Helpline that provides support and information for people experiencing substance use disorders and their families. This line can help connect people with local resources and recovery groups. It can be reached by calling 1-800-662-4357.

Acknowledgments

To my agent, Lauren Spieller, for your continual support—I'm so glad you represent my work.

To my editor, Jenne Abramowitz, for your thoughtful feedback and encouragement during this book's birth. There's so much of myself in Sparrow's story, and I'm grateful every day to be working closely with someone I trust.

To the team at Scholastic who worked so passionately on this book, from the bottom of my heart and on behalf of my readers, thank you for sharing this joy with me.

To the family, friends, and queerdos near and far who compose my own Rainbow House: I love y'all.

To Jenny Solidago Mansell: Thank you for sharing your vision of community-based plant learning, and for your love and support.

To David Levithan, for your kindness and encouragement of my work.

To my writing pals: You all rock my world. Special thanks to those who offered feedback and encouragement during the sometimes-emotional process of writing such a personal story. Your memes are sublime.

My magical kids: You are my heart. Thank you for your patience and thoughtfulness while I worked on this project (even if I appreciate your passion for the natural world). Thank you for sharing your favorite animal facts with me and giving me a front-row seat to your fascinating lives.

My readers: You deserve all the goodness and joy that life has to offer. Thank you for the stories you've shared, and for all your love and support. I think about you with great love, every single day.

About the Author

ASH VAN OTTERLOO is the author of *A Touch of Ruckus* and *Cattywampus*, an Indies Introduce and Indie Next pick. When they're not writing or freelance editing, they love gardening, hiking, exchanging playful banter, and collecting folklore stories. A former resident of the Smoky Mountains, they now live in Bremerton, Washington, with their family and an enormous collection of plants.